"Go, Rachel!" Pat yelled.

She shook her head, tumbling wet waves of auburn hair into her face. "We'll never make it."

Pat crouched in front of the shattered window, hefted his weapon and aimed it at the man moving much too quickly toward his cabin. Maybe he could intimidate him and his friends enough to send them on the run. "Freeze!"

The guy lifted his weapon. Pat whipped to the side an instant before the man fired and tore a chunk out of the windowsill.

Jane was curled in a ball in the middle of the floor, arms covering her head, and Shadow, his K-9, crowded against her.

Rachel aimed out the window and took a shot. Distress radiated from her, though she seemed steady enough and held her weapon in a firm grip. "What now?"

"Stay down." If there was a way to get them out of there without hurting anyone, Pat would...but it didn't look promising.

Deena Alexander grew up in a small town on eastern Long Island where she lived up until a few years ago and then relocated to Clermont, Florida, with her husband, three children, son-in-law and four dogs. Now she enjoys long walks in nature all year long, despite the occasional alligator or snake she sometimes encounters. Her love for writing developed after the birth of her youngest son, who had trouble sleeping through the night.

Books by Deena Alexander

Love Inspired Suspense

Crime Scene Connection
Shielding the Tiny Target
Kidnapped in the Woods

Visit the Author Profile page at LoveInspired.com.

KIDNAPPED
IN THE WOODS

DEENA ALEXANDER

LOVE INSPIRED SUSPENSE
INSPIRATIONAL ROMANCE

LOVE INSPIRED® SUSPENSE

INSPIRATIONAL ROMANCE

ISBN-13: 978-1-335-58783-1

Recycling programs for this product may not exist in your area.

Kidnapped in the Woods

For questions and comments about the quality of this book, please contact us at CustomerService@Harlequin.com.

Love Inspired
22 Adelaide St. West, 41st Floor
Toronto, Ontario M5H 4E3, Canada
www.LoveInspired.com

Printed in U.S.A.

I have blotted out, as a thick cloud, thy transgressions,
and, as a cloud, thy sins: return unto me;
for I have redeemed thee.
—*Isaiah* 44:22

To my brother, Chris.
You are with me always.

ONE

Creeping around the dilapidated shack in the woods bordering the Great South Bay in the middle of the night with a blizzard on the way and no backup was downright foolish. She never should have agreed to it. Wouldn't have, if the request hadn't come from Shannon, a frightened fifteen-year-old runaway Rachel had interviewed for a humanitarian piece about homeless teenagers a year ago. She'd connected with the young girl and given her a business card with instructions to call if she ever wanted help. Knowing how fearful Shannon was of authority, Rachel hadn't expected to hear from her, but she must have done something to earn the girl's trust since she kept the card and had finally reached out, her harsh whisper trembling.

Rachel checked her watch. Could it really have been less than an hour ago that Shannon had called, terrified for her missing friend—whom she'd referred to only as Jane, though Rachel had no clue if that was her real identity?

Although Rachel's first concern at the moment had

to be for Jane, whose life was in immediate danger, she couldn't help fearing for Shannon's safety as well. If her current boyfriend—for lack of a better term for the loser she'd hooked up with—found out she'd overheard his conversation and relayed the information to Rachel, there was no doubt in Rachel's mind that Shannon would turn up missing as well. And if Shannon's information was accurate, which Rachel had no reason to doubt, her boyfriend, Alec, should be showing up anytime now with a more than likely unconscious Jane in tow ready to be sold to the highest bidder. But if Rachel intervened, and the men involved looked for the leak, it wouldn't be too difficult for Alec to figure out Shannon had been eavesdropping.

So, Rachel did exactly as Shannon instructed, even forgoing calling the police at her insistence. Though she'd only agreed to that because Shannon wouldn't give her the information unless she did. Besides, even if there had been time, which there wasn't, and even if she was sure of Shannon's information, which she couldn't be, it's not like the police hadn't failed Rachel in the past.

And now, Rachel Davenport was in trouble. Big trouble.

Sweat dripped down Rachel's back, despite the freezing temperature, as she crouched behind a skimpy bunch of branches and twigs that during summer months might have been a bush and actually offered some cover. As it was, if either of the two armed men dragging the slumped teenage girl toward the shack door glanced in her direction, they'd surely spot her and open fire.

Rachel sank lower, hoping the cover of darkness would be enough to shield her presence. She had to make an impossible choice. Risk being caught by turning on her cell phone to check for service and call for help, or chance losing the sixteen-year-old girl the men were currently hauling into the shack to backtrack through the woods and call the police from a safer distance.

The girl's head lolled forward. Scraggly long brown hair hung in limp strands covering her face, so Rachel couldn't tell if she was conscious or not. Although the girl was unusually thin, there was no way Rachel could carry her more than a mile back to where she'd parked the car, even if she could find a way to rescue her.

The low rumble of an approaching engine took the decision out of her hands. Once Jane was sold and disappeared, most likely on the approaching boat, there would be no way to find her again. Rachel already shouldered the responsibility for one girl's disappearance and ultimate death—no way she'd live with the guilt of failing another.

After dumping Jane inside the shack, the two men took up positions on either side of the open door and stood guard, eyes trained on the boat slowing down to dock.

Okay. It was now or never. She couldn't afford to wait any longer, and she didn't have time to go for help. At the moment, there were only two men to deal with. If she waited for the boat to dock, she had no clue how many there'd be. And she didn't plan on hanging around to find out.

She inhaled deeply, the fresh clean scent of the coming storm a reminder she needed to get the girl out of there quickly, and patted the handgun weighing heavily in the holster on her hip to reassure herself it was there—the weapon she always carried for personal protection since her work sometimes put her in dangerous situations, the weapon she'd diligently practiced with on the range but had never fired at another living being. Hopefully, that wasn't about to change. If she could even manage to grip the gun in her frozen fingers, never mind pull the trigger. Keeping the weapon holstered, she inched forward in a crouch, wincing at the crunch of the brittle, frozen leaves carpeting the ground.

One of the men glanced toward her.

She held her breath and lowered her face, willing herself invisible.

He continued to scan the area for a moment, then returned his attention to the boat with at least two men on board.

The breath shot from her burning lungs, and she lowered herself to the ground, lying flat on her stomach. As stealthily as possible, she crept forward, resisting the urge to move faster.

Half the boards on the shack's walls had rotted away, and most of the windows were broken. If she could circle around the back of the building, she might be able to get to the girl and get her out without being seen. How she'd get her from the shack back to the dirt road where she'd parked the car, she had no idea. But she'd cross that bridge when she came to it. *If* she came to it.

Trying to stay completely quiet, she inched forward.

She took shallow breaths, wishing there was something she could do about the puff of vapor that accompanied each exhale. The odor of mold, dirt and dried leaves tickled her nose as she belly-crawled toward the side of the building, keeping her head low, resisting the overwhelming urge to sneeze.

The instant she was out of view of the guards, she sat up and scooted her back against the shack's side wall, then paused to take a few deep breaths of the frigid air. Between her heart hammering against her ribs and the lungful of ice-cold air, her chest ached.

The sound of the engine grew louder.

As she peeked around the corner, a light shone across the front of the shack from the bay, illuminating the guards.

They started across the clearing toward the dock, their attention drawn away from her.

Knowing it might be her last chance, Rachel shoved herself to her feet and bolted around the back and onto a rotting deck. A broken sliding door allowed a view through the interior of the shack and out the front windows. She tried the door. Locked. She reached in through the broken glass, fumbled around for the latch and released the lock. With a clock ticking away in her head, she yanked her arm out too quickly, slicing the back of her hand.

She almost cried out, caught herself just in time and hissed a few breaths through her teeth. The door didn't slide open easily, but she managed to wrestle it open far enough to squeeze through, wincing when it squeaked. Thankfully, the guards had walked far enough toward the dock, and the wind had picked up enough to cover the sound. Rachel called out in a harsh whisper. "Jane."

The wind carried the sound of men's raised voices to her. They were coming back. She was out of time.

"Jane. *Psst.*"

Nothing. With the front door open and the light from the boat that was now docked shining into the shack, she could barely make out the silhouette of the girl lying on the floor beside the doorway.

She hurried across the open room, the boards groaning loudly beneath her footsteps. When she reached Jane, she knelt beside her and pressed her fingers against the girl's neck, then breathed a sigh of relief at the strong pulse. Rachel covered Jane's mouth to keep her from getting startled and crying out, then shook her arm and whispered, "Jane."

As the girl jerked away, her eyes shot open.

Rachel put a finger against her lips.

Jane nodded, her gaze skipping frantically around the room, out the front door and then back to Rachel.

Trusting the girl would remain quiet, Rachel removed her hand and gestured for Jane to move toward the back door.

She got as far as her hands and knees, then swayed. Drugged? Injured? Rachel didn't know, and there was no time to find out now. "Can you stand?"

Jane didn't answer, just fisted her hands against the floor.

Rachel's heart ached to slow down, comfort the girl, assure her everything would be okay. But it wouldn't be. Not unless she could get her out of there without drawing any attention. Her mind begged her to shove all compassion aside and move faster. She risked a quick peek out the front window. Bathed in the light cast from the boat stood six men. Four more had joined the two she'd already seen, presumably from the boat. Rachel started to turn away, but a familiar form caught her attention.

Ben Harrison. She'd recognize his stride anywhere, though the confident swagger she'd once found endearing, comforting even, now seemed more like an arrogant strut. For just a moment, her heart soared. Even if they hadn't spoken in years, surely Detective Harrison would help her and Jane out of this mess. Although, if he was undercover, she could be putting him in danger too. Unless…

She and her cousin Ben had been so close once upon a time. Growing up, he'd been her best friend, her confidant, the one person she trusted with all her heart. And then he betrayed her at the time she needed him the most. He'd taken up with a bad crowd and blown her off when she'd begged him for help finding her sister, Rebecca, when she went missing. Then, when Rachel had nowhere else to go for help when the police botched the investigation into Rebecca's disappearance, he'd turned her away. Her parents assumed Rebecca had run away and gave up on her, retreated into themselves until it was too late to save her. And in abandoning Rebecca, they'd all abandoned Rachel as well, leaving her with no one to depend on but herself.

When she heard he'd joined the police academy and then made detective, she'd hoped he'd left the bad crowd behind him, turned over a new leaf. She even held out hope he might reach out to her one day, apologize. Not that it could change what had happened with Rebecca. A niggle of fear crept in, raised goose bumps, and she slid deeper into the shadows.

As Ben strode straight toward the shack barking orders, the others fanned out behind him. But if Ben was undercover, why would he appear to be the one in charge? She'd stopped talking to him years ago because she didn't trust him. No sense changing that opinion now.

"Come on, Jane. We have to go." She grabbed Jane beneath the arm and hauled her up to stand. "Now."

Jane staggered but stayed on her feet as Rachel propelled her toward the door through the narrow gap she'd managed to open and out onto the deck. Hopefully, the cold air would help Jane regain her senses enough to run.

All they had to do was make it across the clearing and they could disappear into the heavily wooded Pine Barrens. Maybe. Flurries started to fall, fat white flakes drifting lazily to the ground. A deceptive start to the forecast storm that would soon grip Long Island in its bitter fury.

With a firm hold on Jane's wrist, Rachel hurried across the deck and started through the stiff dead grass, ignoring the loud crunching sound each footstep made. The girl's captors would be on them any minute. Stealth wouldn't do them any good now. Only speed might save them.

Rachel started to run, prodding Jane to move faster, half dragging her by the arm.

A gust of wind carried the sounds of raised voices. A man shouted from inside the shack.

Jane stumbled.

They weren't going to make it to the tree line, and there was nowhere to hide in the open clearing.

"Run straight for the woods. Go." She shoved Jane forward. "Now."

Dazed, Jane glanced over her shoulder toward the shack. Her eyes went wide, and tremors tore through her. Like a deer caught in headlights, she froze, vulnerable.

Six black-clad figures emerged from the shack with Ben in the lead.

The two men who'd been guarding Jane flanked him with their very large guns trained on Rachel and Jane.

Ben poked a finger against one man's chest. "You were paid to watch her, not dump her in an unsecured shack so she could escape."

"But we drugged her." Keeping his weapon level, trained on Rachel, the man turned his head toward Ben. "She was out cold a minute ago."

"Yeah, well, she's not now, is she?" Ben pointed his weapon at the man's chest and fired.

The man crumpled to the ground.

Rachel wheezed in a breath.

"Hey." The other man started backing up, his gun still aimed at the women. "Hey, dude, I was just the—"

Ben's second gunshot dropped the man midsentence. Ben gestured for one of the men to go back toward the front, then started forward with the remaining three. "We need the girl alive."

Bile surged, burning the back of Rachel's throat. He'd just killed two men. Two of his own men.

She turned to Jane, gripped her shoulders and stared into her unfocused eyes. She shook her once, hard. "You have to run."

The girl nodded, her eyes seeming to clear a little, then turned and fled toward the woods.

Rachel yanked her weapon from the harness as she ran after Jane.

More shouts reached her. The men were almost on them. She was going to have to turn and fight.

A shot rang out.

Jane went down hard on her stomach, barely getting her hands under her in time to catch herself.

No, no, no! "Are you hurt?"

Jane didn't answer.

Crouching beside her, Rachel searched desperately for an escape route.

Another shot hit a tree not far from them. Either the gunman was a lousy shot, or the two shots fired so far had been meant as a warning, which was probably the case. If Shannon was correct, and she had been so far, and Jane was set to be sold, the girl was worth too much money for them to shoot to kill. And Ben had said to take the girl alive. He hadn't said the same about her companion. In the darkness, made even more so by the thick cloud cover and the flurries, they most likely couldn't tell the two apart. Once they got closer and that changed, Rachel would be expendable.

Another shot sent Jane scrambling to her feet and

bolting toward the woods. It seemed the bullets whizzing by her had finally cleared some of the stupor.

Rachel followed, keeping her head down.

Shouts followed them, along with the sound of a car engine turning over. Ben must have sent the guy to get the SUV out front. It would only take a few seconds for them to make it around the small shack to the clearing and join the others chasing them on foot. She had to try to stop them. Or at least slow them down.

Jane dove behind a tree.

"Keep going. I'll be right behind you."

The plea for God's help popped unbidden into her head. She caught herself, remembering the last time she prayed, begged God to return her sister safely, He hadn't answered. It had been more than fifteen years since Rachel had prayed, and if only for her own sake, she wouldn't pray now. How could she ask God to help her after she hadn't trusted Him in so long, after she'd turned away from Him at the moment she'd probably needed faith the most? *Please, help me save this child. I failed Rebecca. Please, don't let me fail Jane.*

Despite her hand shaking wildly, Rachel crouched beside the tree and aimed her weapon. She could do this. She had to. Inhaling deeply, she waited for the SUV to round the corner, then sucked in a deep breath, held it and aimed straight at the front of the SUV now barreling toward her. She squeezed the trigger, heard the sound of the bullet striking metal. Gunfire split the night air as the three men running toward her opened fire.

Rachel ignored it, aimed at the guy closest to her and shot him.

If his moans were any indication, she hadn't killed him. Thankfully. She didn't know if she could live with another death on her conscience. It was bad enough she hadn't been able to save Rebecca.

As the wounded man fell, Ben and the other guy fled for cover, barreling into the woods on the sides of the clearing. The SUV stopped where it was—whether because it was disabled in some way or the driver was awaiting instructions from Ben, she had no idea.

And she wasn't hanging around to find out. Not wanting to wait for them to regroup, Rachel turned and ran after Jane. It was easy enough to follow her footprints in the light dusting of snow that had already accumulated. A fact that would be a problem as soon as their attackers got their act together.

She couldn't think about that right now. Couldn't think of anything past this moment. She found Jane leaning against a tree, sucking in deep lungfuls of the frigid air and coughing.

How was she going to get the girl to safety? Her car was on the other side of the shack. She couldn't very well turn around and go back. She had to assume the men who'd dove into the woods for cover would be coming after them, probably flanking them, so there was no way to circle around. The thought that even if she somehow managed to lose the men, they could easily find her car and identify her began as a small niggle at the base of her neck, but she shoved it aside. One catastrophe at a time.

She gripped Jane's arm, keeping her voice barely above a whisper. "We have to keep going."

When Jane looked at her and nodded, her big brown eyes filled with the same terror Rachel felt, her heart broke. She wanted nothing more than to stop for a moment, reassure the young girl everything would be okay. She didn't have that luxury. Stopping now would be a death sentence. Who knew? Maybe her death sentence had already been signed.

They started through the woods. There was no way to walk quietly, so they just plowed on, moving as quickly as possible, every footstep echoing through the silent night.

Though the shouting had stopped, the sounds of pursuit moved closer. At least the crunch of their footsteps and harsh, ragged breaths allowed Rachel to keep track of their progress.

The frigid air burned Rachel's lungs. Tears leaked out of her eyes and froze on her cheeks. The bitter cold stung her face, and her toes had gone numb what seemed like hours ago. Their time was up. If they didn't find shelter soon and couldn't get help, they weren't going to make it.

She inhaled deeply and fought the urge to cough. The faint scent of smoke filled her lungs. A forest fire? Probably not. Surely she'd see the telltale glow of flames if that were the case.

The smoky odor increased. Light flickered ahead in the woods. A fire after all? No. A small A-frame cabin sat amid a circle of grass. Hope surged. Had God answered her prayer for help this time?

She pointed toward the cabin and signaled Jane to run ahead. Rachel ducked behind an SUV parked out front. Using the vehicle as cover, she aimed at the section of woods where the sounds of pursuit were coming from. She struggled to regulate her breathing, slow her racing heart. If she could just buy Jane time to find help.

Ben Harrison burst from the woods, gun held ready. He looked right at her. A spark of recognition flared in his eyes before he shuttered them and took aim.

She didn't want to shoot him. Didn't want to make that choice. She'd loved him once, probably still did, in spite of the pain, anger and sting of betrayal. How could she shoot Ben? Could she kill her own cousin? And for the second time in fifteen years, she prayed. *Please don't let me have to do this.*

Her hesitation gave Ben the upper hand. He squeezed off a shot. It hit a tree not a foot from her head. Splinters of bark ricocheted into her cheek.

She knew Ben was an excellent shot since he was the one who'd taught her to shoot and spent hours on end at the range helping her improve. Had the increasing wind or the instant of recognition for a family member he'd once loved thrown off his aim? Or had he missed on purpose?

Was that a gunshot? Patrick Ryan frowned at the sound muffled by the cabin's heavily insulated walls and the noise of the fire crackling in the fireplace. Probably a hunter. Weird that someone would be out there in the coming weather. Perhaps a hunter had gotten lost. Or maybe Pat had been mistaken, and that troublesome raccoon had gotten into the garbage pails again. No matter what Pat rigged to keep him out of the cans, the sneaky rascal managed to get past it. Not that he blamed the poor fellow for being hungry in the middle of winter, but he was getting tired of picking up the mess.

Shadow, Patrick's Bernese mountain dog, paced back and forth across the front of the cabin, his nails clicking rhythmically against the reclaimed barnwood floors. With an occasional pause to sniff, first at the front door, then at the windows, he continued his restless patrol. Even though the behavior was a little odd for the well-trained rescue dog, Pat wasn't too concerned. Since he'd been there recuperating from the injuries he'd sustained when he fell from a ladder while fighting a house fire, he had seen an occasional hunter or avid hiker in the area. And he'd thought he'd just heard a shot fairly close by. Probably just a deer hunter hoping to catch something before the storm.

Pat didn't often get to spend time in his uncle's cabin in the secluded expanse of woods where he'd spent many childhood summers, but he'd needed the seclusion to heal, to pray, to reexamine his life choices and to decide where to go next. More and more lately, he'd begun to think his path led out of Seaport.

Shadow stopped, barked twice and resumed his pacing.

Pat took his time getting up from the recliner, where he'd fallen asleep in front of the fireplace. A glance out the front window showed the snow had already begun. No problem for him though. The cabin was well stocked, and he had plenty of firewood. Besides, maybe the coming storm would bring the sense of peace that had eluded him since he was injured. Perhaps he'd finally figure out what direction his life was headed.

He didn't rush as he crossed to the door. Although his injuries had mostly healed, he still suffered from stiffness after he'd been sitting still for a while. "What's the matter, boy? Is that pesky raccoon—"

Gunfire shattered the quiet night. No doubt about it that time. Machine gun fire, not hunting rifles.

"Shadow, down."

The big dog obeyed the command, dropping to his belly instantly.

Pat squatted beside him, one hand on his back to offer comfort while he tried to figure out what was going on. Too many shots to be hunters. With the racket going on outside, every critter within ten miles had probably fled.

Confident Shadow was low enough to be out of the line of fire, Pat cracked open the front door intent on peeking out.

A young teenage girl tumbled into his arms. Tremors tore through her, and her arms, bare and covered in scratches in the thin T-shirt she wore, were ice-cold. A tinge of blue ringed her lips.

He caught her before she could hit the floor and eased her inside, then toed the door shut behind him. "Are you hurt? Can you tell me what happened?"

She stared at him without answering, her pupils constricted. Drugs? As a firefighter and EMT for Seaport Fire and Rescue, he'd responded to his share of overdoses, even in the small town. Was that what the gunfire was all about? A drug deal gone bad? With the miles of wilderness surrounding them and easy access to the nearby bay, it wouldn't surprise him. Her pulse was strong, but he needed to get her warm, get his medical kit and check her more thoroughly.

Another gunshot tore his gaze from the girl out the window to the front yard where a dark figure crouched behind his Jeep.

"Shadow, come." With the dog at his side, he lifted the girl and carried her to the couch, then laid her down and tucked a blanket over her. "Wait."

Though he hadn't put Shadow's work vest on, he would still obey the command to stay with the victim until Pat returned.

The girl still didn't respond, simply stared at the wood-beamed ceiling, her teeth chattering.

Leaving her where she was, with Shadow sitting beside the couch, Pat grabbed his cell phone, stuffed his feet into his work boots and yanked his shotgun from above the mantle. The girl clearly needed medical attention, and he wasn't going to get an ambulance out to the cabin nestled on the outskirts of a large section of Pine Barrens. Not with a blizzard in the forecast. Even if he could get service to call for help, which at the moment he couldn't. He dropped the phone into the pocket of his flannel shirt. He had to get to his Jeep.

Loading the gun, he started for the door. He'd pull around back and load Shadow and the girl into the Jeep there. He reached for the door handle.

A woman shoved the door open, dove through the doorway and practically bowled him over, then slammed the door shut behind her. She whirled toward him with blood smeared amid scratches on her face and dripping from a cut on the back of her hand and a white-knuckled grip on a pistol.

Pat lifted the shotgun. "Drop the weapon."

Her eyes went wide with fear. "I'm sorry. I—"

"Lower the gun. Now."

She stared at her shaking hand as if realizing for the first time she was holding a weapon, but she didn't lower it. "Look. We're in trouble. Please, we need help. Can you call 911?"

Pat's cell service had been spotty at best, and with the incoming storm, he had none. At least he could assume she wasn't one of the bad guys if she was asking him to call the police. "Look, ma'am, I can't—"

A barrage of bullets hit the front of the house, shattering the windows.

Pat tackled the woman to the floor, then propelled her ahead of him. "Move. To the back."

She obeyed instantly. At least, she scrambled on her hands and knees as far as the couch, where she stopped to check the girl.

"Get her up. We have to go out the back." Whatever was going on with these two, now was not the time to stop and chat about it. "How many?"

"Three, I think. Maybe four." She helped the girl roll off the couch and shoved her toward the back door, positioning herself between the girl and the shooters. She lay a gentle hand on Shadow's head and urged him ahead of her.

"Straight out the back and into the woods," he yelled.

She shook her head, tumbling long wet waves of auburn hair into her face. "We'll never make it."

Pat crouched in front of the shattered window, hefted his weapon and aimed it at the man crossing the yard, moving much too quickly toward the cabin. Maybe he could intimidate them enough to send them on the run. "Freeze!"

The guy lifted his weapon, and Pat read the intent in his eyes and whipped to the side an instant before the man fired and tore a chunk out of the windowsill.

Leaving the girl with Shadow, the woman returned to crouch beside him, aimed out the window and took a shot.

"Stay down." Pat didn't like the idea of shooting at anyone. If there was a way to get them out of there without hurting anyone, he would, but it didn't look promising.

The girl lay curled in a ball in the middle of the floor, arms covering her head, Shadow pressed against her.

The woman was on one knee, her back against the wall, practically vibrating with energy. She stared at him through jade green eyes with a burst of gold around pupils dilated with fear. Thick lashes darkened by the heavy wet snow framed her eyes, making them appear even larger. Distress radiated from her, though she seemed steady enough, held her weapon in a firm grip.

More shots hit the house.

Pat turned away from those eyes pleading for answers, aimed toward the woods and opened fire.

Two men fled back into the trees for cover. Another stepped forward and lobbed a Molotov cocktail at Pat's Jeep. The explosion rocked the house, and Pat ducked below the window frame. He only waited a moment to risk a glance out the front window to be sure they weren't planning to firebomb the house. There was no sign of the men who'd fled into the woods, but flames engulfed his Jeep. So much for using it to get the girl help.

The man who'd launched the Molotov cocktail strode toward the house, his pace steady and determined.

Whatever Pat had ended up in the middle of, these guys were not playing around. No good guys would randomly shoot up a civilian's home and bomb his vehicle, no matter what these two women had done. Pat fired again, hoping to scare the man off, then grabbed the ammo box and reloaded. Though he didn't want to hurt anyone, he'd have to aim for the man's legs next. He couldn't let him get into the house or get close enough to launch a bomb through the window.

Pat crouched amidst the glass by the front window, held his breath, waited. Had the men gone? Since they'd effectively cut off their only means of escape, unless the woman had a vehicle stashed nearby, they'd probably just retreated for the moment. It would be easy enough to give Pat and the women some room, then come back with reinforcements and get them at the cabin or track them through the snow if they tried to run. He squinted through the broken window, wind battering his face, burning his eyes. No one. Perhaps his gunshots had scared them off.

Either way, right now he had to douse the fire. Between the dried brush and leaves littering the ground and the blizzard force winds headed their way, the entire Pine Barrens would go up in flames if he didn't do something. Even though it had begun to snow, the brush was excessively brittle thanks to a recent dry spell. No way would the little that had fallen so far help stop the fire from spreading.

But what if their attackers were lying in wait? He'd have to be a fool to trust the woman, whose name he didn't even know, to watch his back. But what choice did he have? He held the shotgun out to her. "Take this. It's better than the handgun. You have to cover me so I can extinguish the fire."

"What!" She yanked her hand away. "You can't go out there. What if those guys are still there?"

"I have no choice." He thrust the weapon toward her. "While we're standing here arguing, increasingly strong winds and dead brush are fueling those flames."

She withdrew the weapon gingerly from his hand and took up a defensive crouch, keeping her head low as she aimed out the window. With one deep, shaky breath, she nodded at him. "Go."

With a quick prayer for help, Pat grabbed the fire extinguisher from the front closet and plunged out into the night. Without wasting a minute, trusting the woman to watch for trouble, Pat sprinted up the narrow dirt driveway. Thankfully, the fire hadn't spread beyond what he could handle, and he extinguished it quickly.

But his Jeep was toast. And they still needed to get out of there. While the woman's pursuers might have retreated to regroup or find cell phone service to call for reinforcements, they would undoubtedly return. It was past time to find out what was going on and get the woman and girl to safety.

He ran back to the cabin and shut and locked the front door. Not that it mattered with most of the glass broken out of the windows, but if it bought them even a few seconds, it could be the difference between life and death.

The woman jumped to her feet and offered the weapon. "I'm so sorry. I didn't mean to—"

"Walk and talk." He took the gun from her and crossed the room. They didn't have time to waste. "How about starting with your name?"

"I'm sorry. I'm Rachel Davenport." She hurried next to him but stopped when she reached the girl and squatted down to check on her.

"I'm Pat Ryan. And the girl?" Though he didn't bother changing from his sweats to his jeans, he did pause to tie his boots so he didn't end up face-planting in the snow.

"I think her name is Jane, but I'm not sure."

"You mean you don't know her?" Because he could definitely see law enforcement shooting at her if they suspected she'd taken the girl against her will, though probably not shooting at a random civilian and Molotov-bombing Jeeps. "You didn't kidnap her or anything, right?"

"Of course not. Not really. I don't think so, anyway… but…uh…"

He stopped short and stared at her while she stuttered.

"Actually, she came willingly with me, so I guess it's not kidnapping so much as rescuing her from men who were intent on selling her to the highest bidder." She stood and folded her arms in defiance or maybe because the adrenaline rush was waning and a chill had started to set in. "So I'm pretty sure the police wouldn't view it as an actual kidnapping."

"All right." For the moment, he had to assume she was telling the truth, and she and the girl were both in some kind of danger. "Right now, we need to get out of here before they come back. As it is, I'm surprised they backed off. They could have just bombed the house instead of the Jeep."

"They want Jane alive."

That made more sense. It also meant they'd definitely return.

He didn't have much in the way of clothes at the cabin, since he'd spent much of the past month in pajama pants and T-shirts, but he couldn't allow the girl to walk through the woods in torn jeans and a short-sleeve shirt. She'd freeze to death before they could get her help. Unfortunately, there was nothing he could do about the thin canvas shoes that had worn through one toe. He ran to the bedroom and grabbed a sweatshirt and socks, then handed them to her.

She took them without looking at him.

"Can you tell me your name?" He'd feel better if she could at least confirm Rachel's story.

She didn't answer, so he let it drop. He ran to the kitchen and grabbed Shadow's work harness, slung it over his shoulder just in case, and took a couple of plastic bags and twine from the cabinet beneath the sink. When he returned to the back door, Jane had already pulled on the sweatshirt, put the socks on and redonned her shoes. He bent and tied one plastic bag over each of her feet. Hopefully, it would keep them from getting too wet. Not ideal, but the best he could do under the circumstances. "Okay, let's go. Out the back, straight across the clearing and into the woods."

Rachel nodded. She, at least, was wearing a jacket, though not heavy enough for the coming weather, and she had no hat, no gloves, just jeans and boots. She laid a hand on his. The delicate brush was enough for him to feel how cold her fingers were. It was a wonder she'd ever gotten a shot off. "I'm so sorry I brought trouble to your door, but thank you for helping us."

"Sure thing." He glanced at Jane then scanned the darkness out the French doors while he spoke. "Was she drugged?"

Rachel looked toward her and shrugged. "I don't know. I suspect she was though. When I first saw her, two men were dragging her into a nearby shack. She looked dazed, unresponsive. Maybe unconscious."

"How did you find her?" The steady *tick, tick, tick* of an imaginary clock in his head begged him to get moving, but he needed at least some understanding of the girl's condition if he was going to help her.

"I'll tell you all of it later, but the short version is I'm a journalist. I did a story on runaway girls who've been disappearing, and one of the young teens I spoke with, Shannon, kept my card and called me, said her friend, Jane, was in trouble. Shannon overheard the guy she's been seeing on the phone making arrangements to pick up the girl and meet a boat at the shack they sometimes used for drug deals. She called me right after he walked out the door, but she made me promise not to call the police, said she wouldn't tell me where they were selling and transporting the girls they snatched unless I agreed. So I did."

She lifted her chin as if expecting to have to defend her decision. "I had no choice. If I hadn't left immediately, I'd have missed them. I figured I'd have time to check things out, then call the police if the information turned out to be accurate. But there was no time. The men showed up with Jane not long after I got there, and then the boat arrived to pick her up, and I was afraid she'd be gone if I went for help."

"You realize you're going to have to break that promise now, right?" He couldn't just dump the two of them off somewhere without knowing they had police protection.

She caught her bottom lip between her teeth and lowered her gaze.

"What?" He lowered his voice even further. "You can't think you're going to dump her off somewhere and walk away."

"Of course not. I'm just keeping my options open." She sighed. "Look, you're helping us, and I appreciate that, but there's something you should know. If you don't want to help after that, I'll understand, and we'll get out of your hair."

He waited, let her think through whatever she wanted to share.

"I recognized one of the men who came after us. He's a detective."

So, she admittedly snatched the girl. A detective was

chasing her—a detective Pat had taken more than one shot at. "You think he's undercover?"

"I don't know. Maybe. I saw him shoot two men. But when he had the chance to shoot me right before I ran, he didn't take the shot. Well..." She frowned and shook her head. "He actually took the shot but missed."

Pat grabbed his coat from the closet, helped Jane get it on over the sweatshirt. Then he took her by both shoulders, rubbed his hands up and down her arms. He had to know, needed some acknowledgment from her that she wanted to go with them. Not that he could leave her there either way. "Jane."

She studied his feet.

"Look at me for a moment, Jane."

She was painfully thin to begin with, but the sweatshirt and coat swallowed her up, made her appear so young, so vulnerable. She lifted her gaze to his, her long, stringy hair covering one eye, the other eye sunken in a deep black bruise.

Rage surged through him. "We're going to try to get you help, okay?"

Nothing.

Rachel laid a hand on her shoulder, seeming to understand his need for approval. "Jane. Do you want to come with us?"

She glanced at Rachel from the corner of her eye and nodded once.

That was all the confirmation Pat needed. "Let's go."

Moving quickly, he put out the fire he'd been enjoying what seemed like hours ago and eased open the back door. A blast of cold air ushered in a torrent of snowflakes. He left the lights on. If the attackers thought they were still inside when they returned, which he had no doubt they would, it might slow them down for a few minutes while they checked things out. Especially if they approached carefully, wary he and Rachel would open fire from the cabin again.

"Stay against the back of the house, move to the corner, then when I give the signal, run straight for the woods."

Rachel kept her weapon in one hand and held Jane's hand in the other.

With Jane's free hand, she kept a tight grip on Shadow's collar.

Fat, wet snowflakes swirled and churned. At least the storm would give them some cover since visibility was practically nonexistent. But it would make it harder for them too. They could run right into their attackers before they even saw them. "Go straight until you come to the beach, then we're going to walk along the water's edge."

Rachel frowned in the direction he'd indicated. "Why don't we stay in the woods? Wouldn't that give us more cover?"

"They'll expect us to do just that." It was snowing hard enough to cover their tracks pretty quickly, but he didn't want to take any chances of leaving an easy-to-follow trail. He prayed they'd make it to a house quickly, because even if they managed to outrun their pursuers, none of them were clothed or equipped properly to survive this storm. "The nearest town is about fifteen miles through the woods, but if we walk along the shore, we'll come to a stretch of beach lined with summer homes in about two miles. Hopefully, one of them will have left a car or an SUV in the garage."

No one should be in residence this time of year, and even if they had been, there were evacuation orders in place due to the coming nor'easter that would push massive amounts of water onto the shore. His uncle's cabin sat on high enough ground to be safe, but the houses along the beach road didn't. Who knew? The beach might prove to be impassable already. They'd have to deal with that later. For now, the best he could do was get Rachel and Jane somewhere warm and safe and get them whatever medical attention they might need.

At his gesture, the two took off across the field with Pat trying to cover them as best he could. He didn't know where the men had gone, but he expected them to return.

TWO

Rachel stayed behind Jane and Shadow. At least the girl followed directions, even if she wouldn't speak to them, couldn't or wouldn't tell them what had happened to her. And she'd taken to the dog, kept one hand on his head as they walked.

The instant she reached the tree line, Rachel chanced one quick glance across the clearing to be sure Pat was following.

He waved her forward, then turned and scanned behind them. Apparently satisfied the men hadn't yet returned, he fell into pace beside Rachel with Jane and Shadow walking ahead of them into the woods.

The cold had already seeped all the way down to Rachel's bones, and they still had at least a couple of miles to walk. Though the coat Pat had lent Jane swallowed her up, it should keep her warm. But Rachel was worried about Jane's feet in the ripped canvas shoes, despite the thick socks Pat had given her and the plastic bags he'd tied over her shoes to keep them dry. Frostbite was a good possibility. The poor girl had to be terrified.

Rachel pitched her voice low so as not to frighten Jane further. "Do you think they'll come after us?"

Pat glanced over his shoulder.

Rachel followed his gaze to the trail of footprints they were leaving behind them.

"Yeah, they'll come. You said the detective saw you. Do you think he recognized you?"

As much as she'd love to believe he didn't, there was no way. She'd met his gaze, and she'd seen the spark of recognition in his eyes, the instant of surprise. "He recognized me."

"Okay, then he probably knows you recognized him as well."

"So why did they run off?" Rachel figured they were finished once the shooters approached the cabin, more than willing to kill an innocent bystander to retrieve the girl. But they'd turned and fled rather than killing everyone to get her. A small spark of hope had lit in her.

"Sorry, but it's likely they'll come after us. Why go up against us when we were armed and had the cover of the house when they could just fall back, regroup, bring in reinforcements and easily follow our trail? They've successfully eliminated my vehicle and either eliminated or cut off access to yours, so we have no choice but to run on foot. And if you're right and the detective knows who you are, he probably figured even if we managed to escape these woods…"

The expression in his eyes told her he had his doubts about that. "He'd know where to find me whenever he was ready."

"Exactly."

"And he'd probably assume I'll be afraid to go to the police." Or wouldn't trust them. Ben knew full well the police hadn't helped them find Rebecca before it was too late. Rachel's shoulders slumped with the weight of responsibility.

Pat didn't say anything.

She watched Shadow trot at Jane's side, keeping pace with her, then glanced at Pat, jaw clenched in concentration…or pain… He seemed to be limping. Oh, man, had he been injured, and she hadn't even noticed? "Are you okay? Were you hurt?"

He waved off her concern. "I'm fine. I was injured in the line of duty last month."

She froze dead in her tracks. Could he be in cahoots with Ben? She'd been so relieved to find help when she needed it that she hadn't given any thought to the fact that this man was holed up in a cabin in the woods with a blizzard moving in. "You're a cop?"

He stopped and looked back at her, then frowned. "A firefighter."

"Oh." Relief sent a chill rushing through her. She started to walk again. They'd have to pick up the pace if they were going to get out of there. "I'm sorry to hear you were injured. And I'm so sorry I got you into this mess. I guess you were in the wrong place at the wrong time, and I feel awful for involving you."

"Hey." He laid a hand on her wrist, stopping her. At the speed Jane was moving, they'd easily catch up. "Listen to me. It's fine. I just consider it a blessing I was there to help."

He left the rest unfinished, for which she was grateful. No need to say what they both already knew. If not for running into him, she would surely be dead and Jane gone, beyond help. Ben Harrison may not have been ready to take on both of them, but if he was dirty, he'd keep coming for her. Most likely, he was putting together the manpower to come after them while letting them exhaust themselves and possibly freeze to death in the process. A shiver raced up her spine.

Pat started walking again, looked over at her and grinned, a spark of mischief in his deep blue eyes. Snowflakes caught in his shaggy dark blond hair and short beard. Seemed Pat Ryan was probably quite charming under better circumstances. "Besides, you could see it as me being in the right place at the right time."

A laugh slid out, surprising her that she could find any humor in their current dire circumstances. "I suppose that's one way to look at it."

She could also look at running into him as an answer to the prayer she'd so desperately uttered. Considering that, she offered a silent prayer of thanks. She found peace in prayer as she strode through the deepening snow as they left the cover of the woods to walk along the open beach grass–covered dunes, as she asked forgiveness for turning away for so many years. If she was going to die, she wouldn't do so on bad terms with her Savior.

Wind howled, waves crashed against the shore, and the bay that had already surged across the beach now forced its way over and between the dunes. Snow swirled around them. Yet, even with at least one killer on their heels, the peace that came with a snowstorm, the feeling of isolation and solitude, brought a sense of comfort.

Images of Pat snuggled beneath a blanket in his recliner, the cozy fire blazing for warmth, with Shadow curled by his side invaded her mind. "What were you doing out here, anyway? This deep in the woods in the dead of winter? Hunting?"

"Recuperating."

"In a secluded cabin with a blizzard coming?"

"I needed the peace." He paused, and she wondered if he'd elaborate, if he would share what could have driven him to crave solitude. "And I had everything I needed at the cabin: wood for the fire, plenty of food and water, a generator."

"Oh." If possible, she felt even worse for disturbing him, for putting his life in danger, destroying his vehicle and his cabin. "I'm sorry."

"Don't be. It was time for me to get moving anyway. They say God works in mysterious ways. Maybe this was His way of giving me a boot in the behind." His smile was infectious. "I've been mostly healed physically for a while now, but I've been rethinking my choices of late, trying to decide if I want to continue volunteering with Seaport Fire and Rescue or move on to something else."

She smiled—she couldn't help it—and shook her head. "And did our intrusion sway you at all one way or the other?"

"Honestly? I think maybe it did."

"Really?" She didn't know why that surprised her.

Probably because she couldn't figure out when he would have had time to think rationally about anything but survival since she and Jane had crashed through his front door and into his life.

"Well, since my day job as an IT tech has me sitting behind a computer all the time, one of the things I've been considering is the danger involved in being a volunteer firefighter, even in the volunteer work I do with Shadow at Seaport Search and Rescue." He paused for a minute, frowned.

"And then you ended up in a life-threatening position while sitting peacefully in a cabin in the middle of the woods, where no one should have been around for miles." She could see where he might take that as an indication of what path he was meant to follow.

"Exactly." He shrugged and increased his pace. "Sure does make you wonder, doesn't it?"

That it did. She scanned the empty beach around them as she hurried to keep up with him. Waves crashed into the dunes, one after another fueled by the storm, each sending up a spray of foam and water. "Did you see something?"

He frowned again, looked around. "No, did you?"

"No, but you've picked up the pace considerably in the past few minutes. And Shadow walks faster when you do, prodding Jane to keep up with him."

He nodded. "Shadow's used to hiking in the woods and on the beach with me. He usually runs ahead, then comes back, enjoying a romp in the leaves and brush, digging up sticks and driftwood in the sand. He knows the difference between a playful walk and working a mission. The fact that he's sticking so close makes me think he senses something's wrong. It could be whatever injuries the girl has. Or it could be something else."

A small flicker of guilt tried to surface. "I wish I would have been able to examine her before I yanked her out of that shack and forced her to run, but there just wasn't time."

"It's okay. You did what you had to. As soon as we can find some kind of shelter, I'll take a look at her more closely."

"Do you know what to look for?"

"I do. I'm trained as an EMT as well as a firefighter."

Rachel didn't believe in luck, so she could only trust that Patrick Ryan had to be a blessing, an answer to her prayer. She'd need to take some time to consider that if they ever got out of this mess.

"But for right now, let's see if we can get her to move faster. We need to find shelter and get out of this weather."

Rachel continued to put one foot in front of the other, keeping her head low. Bitter wind-whipped snow scathed her cheeks. Sand shot up with each incoming wave. It felt like her face was being sandblasted. She kept her hands in her pockets, the gun clutched in a firm grip, though she was pretty sure her hand had just frozen in that position, and she wouldn't even be able to pull the trigger if need be. Her teeth began to chatter.

She lifted her head and looked over the large expanse of bay. The snow swirled like a million stars against the blackness, creating the illusion she was hurtling through space. She squinted to decrease the effect.

Pat laid a hand on her arm. "Up ahead."

She looked in the direction he pointed, but all she could see was snow. "What is it?"

"The summer homes. Come on." He moved past Jane and into the lead.

Rachel tried to walk faster, but her feet wouldn't cooperate. She needed to be somewhere warm. Needed to sit down for a minute. She was pretty sure her feet would be killing her if not for the fact they were frozen solid in her boots. Her thighs ached from trudging through the sand and snow, which seemed to be growing deeper by the minute. And she had a pounding headache, probably from the fact that her cousin had killed two men and might this moment be lining her up in his sights and exhaling to take his shot.

Pat passed the first mansion they came to. If the killers were following a distance behind, they'd expect him to stop at the first place he saw, especially since the surf was already churning around the stilts the house was built on. With the storm limiting visibility, he couldn't see how many summer homes lined this stretch of beach, but if memory served, there were at least eight or nine. When he reached the second home, he turned up the walkway, trying to put a bit of distance between them and the incoming tide.

"Are we stopping here?" Rachel's shaky voice begged him to do just that, but he wanted to go a little farther.

"Not yet. Let's pass another two, then I'll see if we can get inside."

She hunched over, wrapping her arms around herself, and followed without another word.

Jane had yet to say anything at all, and he was growing more and more concerned as she strode mechanically through the snow.

When they reached the fifth house in line, he led them underneath the stilts the house was built on, where roiling black water had already begun to rise with the tide. "We're going to have to get in and out quickly. I'll break in the back door and unlock the front for you. Once we're inside, I'll take Shadow and check the garage for a vehicle. You two look for a coat closet or bedrooms and see if there are any kind of boots, gloves, hats—anything you can use to keep warm if we have to keep walking."

Rachel nodded.

Jane stared straight ahead. She was no longer shivering.

"We have to be in and out quickly," he reminded them.

Rachel turned her gaze to Jane, then back to Pat. "Can't we at least stay long enough to warm up? If there's a landline, maybe we can call an ambulance."

"Chances are there will be an alarm on the house. It might not sound here since the houses are spaced so far apart and there's no one around to hear it if it does go off, but it will most likely be connected to a service. They'll call the house first to make sure it wasn't a mistake, but when we don't answer or answer and don't have the code, they'll notify the police."

Jane stiffened. Her fear-filled gaze shot toward Pat, and she clenched her teeth, though she remained silent.

"And if the detective you recognized hears the call, he'll know exactly where we are."

Though he didn't think it was possible for Rachel to pale any further, she did. "Okay, you're right."

Jane slumped against one of the pilings.

"Are you ready?" Pat asked.

At Rachel's nod, he gestured toward the road. "Take Shadow with you, and go around the front to the driveway and up onto the decking. I'll open the front door and let you in."

"What about you?"

"It'll be easier to break in from the back." If he had to break in at all, which he was hoping he wouldn't. Since no one lived in these houses for most of the year, they usually had caretakers to check on things and coordinate workers, but the owners often hid a key for housecleaners and maintenance people to get in. Though he'd return once he got Rachel and Jane to safety to take care of any damages, he'd hate to leave the house with a broken window and at the storm's mercy.

"But the water is already covering the back steps."

"I'll be okay. I'm trained for this kind of stuff. Just get Jane and Shadow up to the front deck. I don't want them wet in case we have to keep walking." Though he didn't think Jane would make it much farther, and he had concerns about Rachel as well. "Let's get this done."

She took the shotgun from Pat and guided Jane and Shadow toward the front. He'd have liked to watch until they were safely on the decking, but the constant nagging in his gut that had kept him from danger more than once prodded him to hurry. It was a feeling he should have listened to while fighting the fire he was injured during—the fire that had claimed the lives of the couple that lived there, the couple he'd been too late, too slow, to save. He'd almost reached them, had them in view, when the world around him exploded, throwing him from the ladder and consuming the building. His fault. All because he'd hesitated, only for a few seconds, an instant of indecision after a floor collapse had injured three of his fellow firefighters not that long ago. If he hadn't paused at the bottom of the ladder, would he have been able to save them? Or would he have died too? He'd never know, but he did know he wouldn't live with that guilt again. He wouldn't fail Rachel and Jane.

He'd only have minutes to get inside once he was wet. All the training in the world wouldn't stave off hypothermia at these temperatures. With that in mind, he plunged down the dune and into ice-cold water up to his thighs. It stole his breath as he fought the undertow that wouldn't be an issue in the usually calm bay. But the storm coming up the coast had waves crashing against the pilings, then sucking the sand out from beneath his feet. No doubt the raging ocean had already breached the barrier island in spots and poured into the bay. He grabbed the stair railing, hoisted himself up and over the side and ignored his body begging him to take a moment to catch his breath. His feet were frozen. Everything ached. It had been over a month while he'd recovered from his injuries that he hadn't done anything more demanding than his physical therapy, and his body screamed in protest. The parts he could still feel, anyway. His feet and legs had already gone numb.

With a death grip on the icy railing to keep from slipping and falling into the bay, he navigated the steps toward the second story as quickly as possible, then crossed the deck to the back door. He found the key in a metal box behind the hose bib and offered up a small prayer of thanks.

He let himself in through the back door on the elevated deck, then left the key on the counter, locked the door behind him and hurried to let Rachel and Jane in. The instant he opened the door, Rachel ushered Jane and Shadow inside.

"Go. See what you can find." He called Shadow to him and headed down the stairs toward the garage. If they could find a vehicle, they'd be able to get help fairly quickly. If not, he might have to reconsider his options and try to find a place to hole up until the storm passed. His hopes were dashed the instant he opened the door to the garage. No cars. But…

Two ATVs stood in one corner of the three-car garage. A row of helmets sat on a shelf above them. While the open vehicles wouldn't offer any protection from the elements, at least they'd be faster than walking. Or would they be better off moving on to the next house and checking for a car or SUV?

He took a large cooler off a rack on the back of one of the ATVs and patted the rack. "Shadow, in."

The dog obeyed instantly. He fit perfectly in the rack. Not ideal, but better than him having to run beside them in the snow. His double coat would keep him warm, but ice had already accumulated on his paws.

They'd take these for now, then see what they could

find. It was better than having to backtrack if they didn't find anything at one of the other homes. He found keys on a hook beside the door and shifted both ATVs to face the garage door. He wouldn't start them until they were ready to leave, since he couldn't leave the garage door open and announce their position, but he left the keys dangling from the ignitions. "All right, come on, boy. Let's go see what Rachel found."

Leaving Shadow's work harness hooked over the handlebar, he jogged up the stairs to the kitchen and found Rachel opening and closing cabinets.

She whirled toward him, hand going to her holster, since the shotgun lay on the counter out of her reach.

"Hey, it's just me. Are you guys ready?"

"Just about." She turned back to the cabinet and pulled out a bowl, then filled it with water and set it on the floor for Shadow. She scooped a pile of clothes from the counter and held them out to him. Again, she'd put someone else's needs ahead of her own, as she still wore her dripping clothes. With that one act, he saw her in a new light. And he had no lingering doubts that she'd done nothing but try to help Jane. "Here, I found these for you. This is essentially a summer home, so there's not much in the way of winter clothing. I don't know if they'll fit, but it's all there is, and you're soaking wet."

Jane sat at one of the chairs, pulling the plastic bags and thin shoes off. A pair of what appeared to be men's work boots, and definitely too big for the petite girl, sat beside her. At least the girl was moving faster. Maybe whatever drugs he suspected they'd given her were wearing off.

Taking the clothes, he opened the first door he saw, which turned out to be a large laundry room, ducked inside and shut the door. He removed his boots and set them aside, since the pair Rachel had found were too small, then quickly changed clothes. The jeans were a little big, but they'd do. He belted them, pulled on two pairs of the dry socks Rachel had brought, then stuffed his feet back into his boots. He dropped the wet clothes on top of the washing machine so they wouldn't damage the hardwood floors. Hopefully, he'd reclaim them when he returned to explain to the owners what had happened, bring the ATVs back and repay them for anything they'd taken or damaged.

Rachel knocked on the door.

"Come in." He zipped the sweatshirt she'd given him over the long-sleeved pullover.

"Here. You should drink something." Rachel handed him a water bottle. "We're ready."

"Did you and Jane have something to drink?"

"We did."

He noticed Rachel still wore her wet jeans and jacket, but she had on borrowed boots. At least her feet would be warmer. "You couldn't find dry clothes?"

She shook her head. "I'll be all right until we get somewhere safe. It mostly didn't soak all the way through. Yet."

"All right, then…" He uncapped the water and slugged down half the bottle. "Let's get out of here. Have you ever ridden an ATV?"

"A few times when I was a teenager." She frowned, her eyes narrowing as she studied him. "Why?"

"Because that's all I could find."

She blew out a breath as she seemed to consider and dismiss the alternatives in a fraction of a second and nodded.

A spark of admiration ignited in him. No matter what happened, she seemed to take it in stride. Not that she indiscriminately followed orders. He'd watched her weigh her options before she agreed to the ATVs, and she'd questioned his reasoning on walking along the dunes instead of staying in the cover of the woods, but she didn't get hung up on making decisions. She didn't hesitate.

He strode to the kitchen and looked around, grabbed the shotgun from the counter. Should they take anything with them? Water, maybe? No. Better to just get moving. Not like there wasn't enough snow out there to keep them hydrated if necessary. Carrying anything would only slow them down. Besides, God willing, it wouldn't take them long to find help now. "Let's get out of here."

Of course, he had no idea where to take them. Not his house. As soon as the detective figured out his uncle owned the cabin they'd fled from, it wouldn't take him long to connect him to Pat. Not a police station. A hospital then? Maybe Seaport Firehouse. Surely his friends would help treat their injuries, help protect them. But did he really want to bring that kind of trouble on his fellow firefighters? Uncertainty beat at him. All he knew was he had to keep them safe, get them help. The thought of failing them was unbearable. He stretched his back, desperate to ease some of the soreness the trek through the cold, damp night had left him with.

Jane once again laid a hand on Shadow's head, the big dog seeming to be a comfort to her, as she started down the stairs to the garage. Rachel was right behind her with Pat bringing up the rear. Before he could contemplate his choices any further, the back windows imploded under a barrage of machine gunfire.

THREE

Rachel ducked, covering her head with her arms. A stab of pain pierced the side of her neck below her ear, and she felt the trickle of blood into her collar. A bullet? Had she been shot?

Her knees buckled, and she grabbed the railing to keep from tumbling down the stairs.

Pat caught her beneath her arm and steadied her while thrusting her forward. "Keep moving."

Bullet or not, she was still on her feet, so she kept going, plunging recklessly down the stairway.

Jane and Shadow had been protected by the open door, and they flew down the stairs ahead of her.

"Here. Stop." Pat gripped Rachel's arm and led her to the back of the garage, then grabbed a clean-looking shop towel from a bin on the tool bench.

Pain tore through her as he pulled a large glass shard from her neck and tossed it onto the tool bench, then pressed the towel against the wound. Keeping the pressure firm, he looked into her eyes. "Are you all right?"

She was so far from all right she couldn't even begin to contemplate it, so she simply nodded and lifted a hand to the compress. As she did, her fingers grazed his warm ones. How had he warmed up so fast? Her hands still felt like popsicles.

He laid his hand against her cheek, searched deep into her eyes. The tenderness of his touch, the fact that he'd take the moment as if chaos hadn't just erupted all around them to be sure she was okay was almost her undoing. "If you can keep moving, we have to go."

She nodded again. He was right. There was no time to linger and contemplate weaving her fingers between his for warmth with who knew how many killers coming after them. "Go. I'm fine."

He studied her another moment, clearly not fully satisfied she was telling the truth, then released her, led her to the ATV and started it for her. "You said you've ridden one of these?"

"Yeah." Exactly twice, one of which ended with her dumped over in a ditch with a broken arm, but no need to share that. Besides, running for your life with killers on your heels was a pretty good motivator. She hopped on, ran through a quick refresher course in her mind at lightning speed. "I've got it."

"Jane will ride with you." He handed Rachel a helmet, then helped Jane put hers on and buckled it.

Straddling the seat behind Rachel, Jane wrapped her arms tightly around her waist.

Rachel fitted her own helmet on, then tucked the compress between it and the wound. It would probably fall off, but it was the best she could do. At the moment, bleeding to death was the least of her worries. At least that would take time. Probably. "What about Shadow?"

"I've got him." He rounded the other ATV and patted the rack on the back. "Shadow, in."

He obeyed instantly.

"Down, boy."

He dropped to lay in the basket.

Though Rachel didn't love the idea of the open vehicles with someone taking shots at them, what choice did they have?

Pat jogged to the button beside the garage door. "The instant it opens far enough to get out, go straight toward the beach. Make sure you stay on higher ground or in the dunes. I'll follow. As soon as we're clear, let me pass you, then follow as close as you can."

She nodded. Blood rushed in her head. The ringing in her ears echoed inside the helmet.

Frigid air ushered a whirlwind of snow into the garage the instant the door began to lift.

She shifted into gear and held her breath as the door lumbered up way too slowly. She already knew their pursuers were out there. Waiting for them to emerge. Would they be shot the instant they left the garage? She wished the door would open faster or that it would just close again, and they could stay safely tucked inside the house until the weather cleared.

"Duck," she yelled to Jane over her shoulder, then thumbed the throttle and lurched forward. Keeping her head low so as not to hit the garage door, she shot from the garage, slid on the icy driveway and regained control as she barreled onto the snow-covered dunes. Not exactly a smooth start, but at least they hadn't been shot yet, so that was a plus.

The mechanics of riding the machine came back to her easily enough as she weaved to avoid the worst of the water washing over the dunes, but she'd never ridden with someone on the back before. Jane's iron grip was making it more difficult to maneuver and to see over her shoulder if someone was coming behind them. Hopefully they'd gotten out before the house was surrounded. Their pursuers wouldn't be able to chase them over the waterlogged dunes with a vehicle, and they wouldn't be fast enough to chase them on foot. Maybe she could actually lose them.

When they reached the next house, which was thankfully set farther away from the water than the last, she wove through the pilings as fast as she dared with the limited visibility. She kept out of the water as much as possible, but each time she hit a small flooded area, the salty water sprayed up, quickly soaking through her clothes and freezing. When the vast darkness of the bay opened up before her, she breathed a sigh of relief and kept to the dunes.

Pat's headlight shone behind and to the side of her.

She moved closer to the water's edge to give him room to pass. Water spurted over them from beneath the tires. Wind howled fiercely, and she was grateful for the protection the helmet offered.

As Pat passed, he gestured for her to follow.

She stayed as close to him as she could while allowing herself room to stop or change direction if need be. Memories of her past chased her through the night, thoughts of another girl she'd made a promise to, her older sister, Rebecca, after she'd disappeared. A promise that still haunted her. A promise that she hadn't been able to keep. If only she'd have been able to convince her parents, the police, even Ben, that Rebecca hadn't run away, things might have turned out so differently, but she'd failed. And she'd spent the past years trying to atone for that, seeking out stories that allowed her to help others, young girls like Shannon. And Jane. Tears streamed down Rachel's cheeks, impeding her vision.

Icy cold water sprayed up from the bay, coating her face shield with ice. She tried to wipe it away with her sleeve, but it smeared, making more of a mess, hazing her vision even worse. She shook off the memories and shifted farther up the dunes toward the woods, still keeping Pat in sight. If she lost him now, she and Jane would probably not make it.

Pat left the beach, returning to the thick Pine Barrens. He threaded his way between towering evergreens, narrowly missing the massive trunks more than once. Although Rachel would have preferred to remain on the beach—even though they were out in the open on the beach, at least she didn't have to worry about plowing into a tree—she followed closely behind. Since she was completely lost, she could only assume the direction Pat headed was probably the most direct route back to civilization.

An engine revved behind her, and Jane's hold loosened for an instant as they both looked over their shoulders.

Two headlights barreled up behind them, one from each side. Dirt bikes? She hadn't seen any dirt bikes in the garage where they'd gotten the ATVs. No wonder the men hadn't shot at them while they were leaving. They must have been busy stealing dirt bikes from one of the other garages along the road.

The fact that Pat and Rachel had a head start probably didn't help much, considering the wide tire tracks they were leaving behind in the snow. The men were gaining ground quickly. Not only were the dirt bikes faster, they also handled better through the maze of trees.

When they reached a clearing, Pat moved aside and waved his hand for her to go ahead. When she pulled alongside him, he pointed across the clearing to a path into the woods.

She nodded, bent low and took off at full speed.

A Jeep leapt into the clearing from a wide path to her right, cutting off their escape route.

She yanked the handles hard to the left and leaned into the turn. Thankfully, Jane leaned with her, then straightened as she leveled out again. They'd have to circle around, get the Jeep to chase them so she could get around it and back to the path that Pat had pointed out. If she could manage that, the Jeep wouldn't be able to follow them onto the narrow pathway.

Pat was on the other side of the clearing, one dirt bike on either side of him trying to cut him off. So far, he'd managed to outrun them, but one of them started to pull ahead.

Rachel set a course straight for the guy on the side closest to her. If he didn't pull away, she'd hit him head-on. She thumbed the throttle all the way, barreling across the field, bouncing and jarring her injured neck, aiming straight for the headlight.

He jerked the bike to the side just before they crashed into each other.

With the woods encroaching, Rachel squeezed the hand brake, slowing to circle around again.

The Jeep barely missed sideswiping her and bounced over a hump in the snow.

Pat kicked out, catching the remaining dirt bike rider still paralleling him.

The bike slid out from beneath the rider, and he tumbled into the darkness.

She shot ahead of Pat and skidded onto the path, almost tipping over when it veered sharply to the left a few yards in. As soon as it straightened out, she rocketed forward, despite the poor visibility. They had to get out of there before their attackers had a chance to regroup.

Pat's headlight beam bounced against the trees, cutting through the darkness. Knowing he was right behind her brought a sense of comfort, a feeling of safety despite the dire circumstances. At least she knew she wasn't alone, didn't shoulder all the responsibility for Jane's safety.

When they finally reached a fork in the path, she pulled aside to let Pat lead, then followed him until they reached a road. Several sets of tire tracks marred the surface of the snow. Pat turned onto the unplowed road and followed the tracks.

Rachel did the same. If they could stay in someone else's tracks, it might make it more difficult to follow them. When they passed a small strip mall, Rachel uttered a prayer of thanks. Civilization, finally, even if all of the businesses were closed.

She stayed close to Pat as he wove his way through a small residential neighborhood, then back through the woods. She wanted to yell after him, ask him why he was heading away from the possibility of help, but all she could do was follow. She didn't know the area, didn't know where to find a police station or hospital, somewhere they could safely seek help. Or could they? If any of Ben's colleagues were involved in whatever he'd gotten himself into, they could definitely be waiting for Rachel and Jane to show up. And she'd have no clue who to trust.

No, better to follow Pat, hope he had some kind of plan. He seemed to genuinely want to help, despite the fact they'd practically forced their way into his home, where he'd been trying to rest and recuperate, with a pack of armed killers in tow.

Pat stopped ahead, and Rachel pulled up beside him. Leaving the ATV running, he lifted off his helmet and approached her, scanning the area as he walked. "We have to get out of this weather."

Rachel nodded. She couldn't agree more.

"There are vacation cabins not far from here. We can hide out in one until the weather clears, then go for help."

Jane stiffened behind her, tightening her grip despite the fact they were sitting still.

Rachel chose her words carefully, not wanting to frighten the young girl any further. "Stopping would be good, but can they find us?"

Pat looked around again. "I doubt it. Once we were on the road, I was careful to follow roads that had tire tracks. And I circled around a number of times. Given the rate at which this snow is falling, all of the tracks should be covered soon enough. I think we'll be safe for the rest of the night anyway. We can reassess once it's daylight."

"Do you think the cabins will have alarms?"

"I've stayed in them before, and the office is alarmed, but the individual cabins aren't. They have a caretaker check them every few days, but I doubt he'll stop in before the weather clears, and we'll be gone by then."

"Okay." She followed him to a cabin at the far edge of the group. They hid the ATVs behind the cabin across the road, left a trail of footprints to the back door and then walked the rest of the way across the road to their cabin, with Pat using a branch to cover their tracks. It didn't take him long to break a small hole in the back window with a rock, shove the shutters open then reach in and unlock it. He boosted Rachel through, and she scrambled over the countertop, lighting her phone's flashlight to guide her across the small, cozy room. Now, if they could just get a few moments' reprieve to figure out what to do next.

Hopefully, if their attackers managed to track them this far, they'd think they'd holed up in the cabin across the road. At least then they might have some warning before their pursuers found them.

Pat didn't love the idea of stopping. If their pursuers knew the area as well as he did, they might think

of the deserted vacation cabins. The extra time he'd
spent trying to shake them and cover their tracks might
not matter.

Unfortunately, they had no choice. The weather had
turned rapidly. Between the pitch-black night, the heavy
windblown snow and the ice and snow caked on their visors, visibility was reduced to practically zero. He had to
stop and assess Rachel's injuries and tend to Jane, either
or both of whom probably needed a hospital. He'd never
had the chance to examine them properly and had no
idea if Jane was injured or what, if any, drugs she'd been
given. Plus, they needed to get in touch with someone
in law enforcement. Even if he didn't take them back
to the firehouse, he could bring them home to Seaport,
only half an hour away in good weather. At least there,
he knew the local police officers, and he could get some
guidance on what to do, who to trust.

The instant Rachel opened the front door, he ushered Jane and Shadow inside and closed the door behind
him, plunging them into darkness, aside from the small
beam of light from Rachel's phone. Thankfully, all of
the windows had been shuttered when they'd closed
up the cabins for the season, and he used his phone's
flashlight to illuminate the dank interior. He flipped
the light switch by the door. Nothing. Either the power
had been turned off for the season, or the storm had already taken down the lines.

Rachel brushed the snow from Jane's hair, then
helped her out of the wet coat and hung it over the back
of a chair at the small table in the kitchenette and ges-

tured for Jane to sit, then turned to Pat. "Do you think it's safe to start a fire?"

Even if they could find dry wood in the small stack he'd seen on the side of the cabin, and even if the storm camouflaged the smoke, the odor would be a dead giveaway if their pursuers detected it. "Better not to, I think."

She nodded. "That's what I figured."

As Rachel pulled out a second chair and sat down to unlace her boots, Pat rummaged through the drawers and came up with a lighter. He lit the two hurricane lamps on the mantle, then took one and set it on the table. The glow from the lamp flickered off the highlights in Rachel's auburn hair, casting a halo of flames around her striking features. There was no denying she was a beautiful woman, despite her hair hanging limp from the wet snow and the dark circles surrounding her brilliant green eyes. Hmm. Beautiful, courageous, selfless… Yup, the exact kind of woman who usually sent him running for the hills. The kind who could suck you in, dig her claws into you and then rip your heart out and leave you a shell of your former self.

He'd thought his mother possessed all of those admirable qualities as well, until the day she'd walked out on his father. Not that he blamed her for that—to say he was a difficult man to live with would be the understatement of the century—but he did blame her for the fact that she'd left a child to live with the man she couldn't.

Pat turned away from Rachel and his past to search for a first aid kit. Beautiful or not, this woman had brought an awful lot of trouble to his door at a time when he should be focusing on figuring out where his life was headed. As much as he loved his work with Seaport Fire and Rescue, he couldn't very well do his job the right way if he was going to second-guess himself every time there was danger. How many lives would be lost while he stood at the bottom of a ladder reliving flashbacks of the frantic search for his fellow firefighters amid a partial condo collapse? Rachel Davenport should be the last thing on his mind right now.

Disgusted with the dark path his thoughts had led him down, he grabbed the second lamp from the mantle and headed to the bathroom. They should be safe enough to lie low in the cabin for at least a few hours and get some rest. Shadow would alert them if anyone approached.

He'd search the cabinets for the kit, tend to Rachel and Jane's injuries, and then it would be time to get some more in-depth answers.

He found the first aid kit in the small linen closet, along with a stack of towels, which he also grabbed. When he returned to the living area, Rachel and Jane sat at the table, coats off, shoes by the door and an afghan from the couch draped over Jane's shoulders. Rachel sat hugging herself and shivering. He hurried to the single bedroom and snatched a blanket from a chest at the foot of a bed, unfolding it as he returned to her.

"Here." He wrapped the blanket around her, then took off his own shoes and coat, and used one of the towels to dry Shadow's thick black coat and another for his paws. When he finally returned to Rachel, the shivering had lessened. Since Jane didn't appear to be injured, aside from an assortment of scratches most likely caused by branches during her trek through the woods, he leaned over Rachel, giving Jane a few minutes to hopefully see he meant no harm. "Let me see your neck."

She tilted her head and lowered the blanket enough for him to see the gash beneath her ear. Blood still trickled from it, but at least the flow had slowed. He cleaned and bandaged the wound, keeping an eye on Jane in his peripheral vision. "We should be safe here, at least for a little while. The shutters will block the dim light cast by the lamps, the ATVs aren't sitting right outside, and whatever signs we might have left will be eradicated by the storm in no time. As long as we don't do anything to draw their attention, we should be okay."

Rachel glanced at Jane from the corner of her eye and frowned at Pat. "Should we take turns resting, in case they find us and we don't hear them?"

"I think we'll be okay. I'm a pretty light sleeper, and Shadow will alert us if they return. That said, I don't want to stay here too long. We should rest and then get out of here, try to get help." A quick assessment assured Pat that Rachel's injuries—the cuts on her face, where branches and twigs had snagged her during her run through the woods, and her hand, which she'd cut breaking into the cabin to rescue Jane—were fairly minor. He started to clean them.

She winced and pulled away at the burn of the antiseptic.

"Sorry." He paused to give her a minute to catch her breath.

"No, it's fine." She relaxed her hand in his hold. "Just get it done."

While he didn't want to frighten either the woman or the girl, he needed to know what he'd gotten himself into if he was going to be able to help them in any way. "Since it looks like we're going to have a little time, why don't you tell me what's going on? All of it, not just the abbreviated version you shared in the middle of a firefight."

A smile played at the corners of Rachel's mouth. "Sorry about that."

He waved it off, enjoying the curve of her lips, the sparkle of the gold bursts in her eyes. "Understood, but I would like some answers now."

She nodded and, to his disappointment, lowered her gaze.

He shook it off. The last thing he needed was any kind of attraction to an unknown woman he couldn't see objectively under the dire circumstances surrounding them. Just because she'd treated the girl kindly, acted selflessly from everything he could see, didn't mean she could be trusted with a man's heart. She was also impulsive, rash and seemed to leap into danger with no thought for her own safety. *Reckless*—that was a good word for her, even if her decisions had been made to save another. What kind of woman would get involved in a mess like this? The kind he should avoid like the plague. But was she the type of woman who would leave an eleven-year-old boy to fend for himself with a man who was too selfish and abusive to see past his own needs and desires?

The last thing Pat needed at the moment, or ever, was a woman to complicate his life. As it was, he'd come to a crossroads, would have to figure out what path he was headed down. And while he had no idea at the moment where that path would lead, the one thing he was certain of was that a white picket fence, 2.2 kids and a happily ever after didn't lie at the end of it. He'd spent his entire life watching his parents destroy each other, and he had no intention of repeating their mistakes. "You've already said you went out there without calling the police because the girl who called with the tip asked you not to. Has your opinion changed?"

"It wasn't only the fact that the girl asked me not to and I agreed, and I would never go back on my word." She glanced pointedly at Jane, seemed to weigh her words carefully. "When I was doing the story about the runaways, I got to know Shannon a little. She's been on her own a long time, and she's…hardened, like she's seen way too much in her years on the street. But when she called me… I can't explain it, but there was something in her voice. Fear, but more. If that makes sense."

Pat only nodded. Done bandaging her injuries, he pulled out the other chair and sat down. He'd need to tend to Jane, but at the moment, the girl sat huddled in the blanket, a look of sheer terror on her face. And he needed a moment to be still. Every muscle in his body screamed at him to rest. The way he felt right now, he wasn't even sure he could still handle firefighting. "You think she knows more than she told you."

"I'm sure of it, but I have no idea what. To be honest, if they'd snatched anyone other than Jane, who Shannon seems to really care for, I don't think she'd have reached out at all."

A tear tipped over Jane's lashes and rolled down her cheek. She hugged her knees to her chest, pulled the blanket even tighter around herself and lowered her head.

"As it is, all she told me was that Alec, her boyfriend, received a call to meet his buddy and take care of the handoff. She said I had to move fast or I'd miss them and to leave the police out of it. I do know she was pretty tight with one of the other teens who went missing last year, because she confided in me when I interviewed her for the story."

Pat stretched his back, twisted from side to side then rubbed his knee, where the dull ache had begun to throb in a steady rhythm. "So what's your plan now?"

Rachel shook her head. "I don't know what to do."

"Who's the detective you were talking about earlier?" Friend or foe?

"His name's Ben Harrison. He's my cousin and was my best friend a lifetime ago. And then...well...something awful happened." She lowered her gaze, but not before he caught the flash of pain. "He started acting strangely. He'd miss get-togethers without calling, spend days at a time out of touch, became short-tempered. I didn't know what he'd gotten involved in, though he had started hanging out with a rough crowd. I thought maybe he was doing drugs, so I looked for any indication that he was."

Understandable, given the circumstances. "And did you find anything?"

"No, nothing. But he continued to grow more and more distant, lie about where he was to his parents, to his former friends, to me. He pushed people away. And when everyone else had given up, I still tried to help him, tried to reach out, tried to understand. Anyway..." When she finally lifted her gaze to his, her eyes had gone cold, empty. Not even a hint of the pain remained beneath the anger burning there. "Then he hit me. Only once, and he seemed to regret it afterward, but it was the last straw. I turned my back on him and walked away. I never saw him again."

"Until tonight."

"Yeah. Until tonight."

"And looking back now, what do you think the problem could have been? Drugs?" Because as a cop, he'd certainly have access, especially if he was dirty. Pat lowered his gaze from hers, didn't want to push her on something she might not be comfortable admitting, even to herself. And yet, they had Jane to worry about, and if Detective Ben Harrison was dirty, he might know exactly where Rachel would run. If he knew her as well as she claimed, it wouldn't be difficult for him to find out her routine. He would already know her friends, family, where she shopped and worked and ate. She'd never be safe. On the other hand, if he was undercover, he could prove to be an invaluable ally.

"You mean, do I think he's dirty?"

Her neutral tone forced him to look at her again if he wanted to gauge her reaction, so he lifted his gaze. "Do you?"

"What happened between us happened when he was

in his late teens at a particularly rough time for my family. If he was on drugs, he'd never have made it onto the police force. But if he wasn't, or if he managed to get off whatever he was taking… Who knows? Maybe he just wasn't ever who I thought he was." She pursed her lips, narrowed her gaze in concentration as if looking back into the past as she seemed to contemplate her answer. "But, in answer to your question, yes, I think it's possible, probable even, that he's dirty."

He glanced at Jane, wondering what her involvement in all of this was.

Then Rachel continued. "When I first started to notice things were off, I didn't make the connection. But, if I'm being honest, the trouble began even before I realized it was a problem. And looking back now, with the advantage of hindsight, the odd behaviors really began when he got involved with Carmine Golino—"

Jane jerked upright, almost toppling herself from the chair, and gripped the table to steady herself.

Rachel frowned. "Jane?"

Eyes wide, she lurched to her feet and backed away from the table.

Shadow scrambled out of the way just in time to keep her from falling over him.

Definitely an unusual reaction. Had it been the name Golino that brought such fear, or had she heard something outside? Pat strained to listen but didn't hear anything other than her harsh breathing and the wind howling against the windows and in the chimney. Shadow stood watching her, and Jane kept her gaze riveted on Rachel.

Pat stood, lifted his hands in front of him in a gesture of surrender. "It's okay, Jane. Whatever's wrong, we're going to help you."

She sobbed, shoved her hair out of her face and uttered the first words she'd said since stumbling through his doorway. "No one can help me."

FOUR

Rachel remained seated at the table, hoping to diffuse some of the tension, terrified Jane was about to bolt. "It's okay, Jane. Whatever's going on, right now, at this moment, you're safe."

Or, at least, as safe as she could be under the circumstances.

"And we're going to do everything we can to keep you that way," Pat added.

"You don't understand." Jane swiped the tears tracking down her cheeks.

"Why don't you sit down and talk to us? Maybe we can help you." And maybe they couldn't, but they'd never know if they couldn't find some way to reach the girl, some way to make her trust them. "And even if there's nothing we can do to help, at least you'd have someone to talk to about the problem. Please."

Jane studied Rachel from the corner of her eye, shifted her gaze to Pat, who still stood facing her, seemingly braced to block the exit if she attempted to flee.

Rachel couldn't blame him, since it was the exact same fear prodding at her.

"Look, Jane." Pat held his hands out to the sides, palms forward. His voice remained calm, reasonable. He'd said he was an EMT and a firefighter; she could easily see where his compassion and confidence would be a comfort to those who'd depend on him. "Even if you don't think we can help, it would be best to sit down and talk about whatever happened. We can't decide how to move forward if we don't know what we're dealing with."

"You're just going to call the cops anyway, so what's the difference?" She took a step back, used the edge of the blanket to shove the tears away then wrapped it tighter around herself. "At least if I keep my mouth shut, I might have a chance of getting out of this mess."

Rachel stood, careful not to move toward Jane, not wanting to spook her into running. "Jane, listen to me, please. You trust Shannon, right? She's your friend. Well, Shannon trusted me. She sent me to find you when you went missing."

"Shannon's a fool. She should have kept her mouth shut." Tremors tore through her slight frame.

"She wanted to help you, Jane." How in the world was she supposed to get through to this girl? She needed help, guidance, something. She had no clue how to deal with a defiant teenager. A quick glance at Pat told her no help was forthcoming, given that he appeared just as confused as Rachel. "She was afraid for you."

"She should have worried about herself. Now, if anything happens to her, it's going to be my fault." Jane fisted her hands, pressed the blanket against her eyes.

Her anguish filled the room, a physical burden that weighed heavily on Rachel's shoulders.

As much as she wanted to help alleviate that guilt for Jane, she couldn't without knowing what the deal was. "So, help us. Help us understand what's going on so we can keep both of you safe."

Jane turned and stared longingly at the cold, empty fireplace as the blanket slid from her shoulders.

Rachel wished they could light it for just long enough to chase away some of the chill, but when she glanced again at Pat, he shook his head. Of course, she'd already known it wasn't a good idea, no matter how damp and cold the cabin's interior. "Please, Jane, sit down and talk to us."

She yanked the blanket tighter around herself. "Why should I trust you?"

"Because when Shannon called me and told me where to find you, and begged me not to call the police, I did exactly what I promised I'd do. I kept my word, Jane." Given Ben Harrison's involvement, that was probably for the best too. "You can trust me. I promise you I'm just trying to help."

Jane turned then, eyed Rachel then Pat. Her expression twisted into one of raw pain. "Why?"

That one simple word, uttered with such aching, broke Rachel's heart. Could this child have been through so much in her short life that a simple act of kindness brought only suspicion? Not that Rachel didn't harbor her own trust issues—God knew she did—but to be so jaded at only sixteen years old? How could that have happened? And in that instant, for just a fraction of a second, Rachel saw a flicker of herself, her own pain, her own mistrust, her own bitterness that had stalked her through her teenage years and into adulthood reflected in Jane. And she knew without any doubt, she'd been called to save this girl. And in saving her, maybe she'd find her own salvation.

"Because I want to help you. I liked Shannon, wanted to help her last year when I met her, but she refused, wouldn't or couldn't trust me enough to allow me in. Until your life was in danger. Then she took a leap of faith and trusted me. Please, I'm asking you to do the same for her." Rachel caught Pat's gaze and, not wanting Jane to feel at all threatened, gestured for him to sit. "Tell us what's going on, then we'll try to find Shannon and see what we can do to save her."

Because Rachel's fear for the girl mirrored Jane's. They had to get to her before Ben and his crew figured out where the leak came from, or the chances of finding her alive were probably slim. Unless Shannon was smart enough to run after calling Rachel. She checked her cell phone. Still no service. She couldn't even try to call the number on her caller ID back and warn her.

"If I tell you what I know, you'll go find Shannon?"

Rachel didn't like that she'd said *you'll* instead of *we'll*. What was she planning to do? She let it go. One problem at a time. And if the girl was willing to talk, no way was she going to nitpick at her phrasing. "Yes. Talk to us, and I promise we'll try to find Shannon."

Jane dropped to her knees on the floor next to Shadow, cradled his head in her lap. "And how do I know you won't go to that cop you know? Your cousin."

Though pain lanced through her at the memories of Ben, she resisted the instinct to close herself off, no matter how badly she wanted to ignore the question. How could she ask Jane to trust her if she wasn't willing to open herself up, share some of her own story, no matter how painful? She couldn't. The only way to earn this girl's trust was to be honest. "One, because I won't betray your confidence. If I make you a promise, I'll keep it. I'm not saying I won't talk to the police at all, but it will only be if we can find a way to do it safely."

"And your cousin?"

"I don't know if I can trust him or not, but either way, I made you a promise, and I won't go back on it."

"You can't trust him," Jane whispered so softly that Rachel had to lean forward to hear her.

For just a flicker of an instant, Rachel wanted to defend Ben. Habit? Maybe. Probably. But she remained quiet.

Jane looked around the room as if to be sure no one else was around, then scooted closer to the table.

Rachel slid off the chair and sat cross-legged on the floor facing her, tunneling her fingers into Shadow's thick fur as she waited for Jane to continue. Tension eased with each stroke. She'd never had a dog of her own and hadn't realized how stress-relieving sitting and petting one could be.

"I know who Detective Ben Harrison is." Jane paused, cast her gaze up toward Rachel.

Since she seemed to be waiting for a response, Rachel chose her words carefully. "What do you mean, you know who he is?"

"I've seen him before."

The memory of Jane's discomfort when she'd mentioned Carmine Golino flashed through Rachel's mind. "You've seen him with Golino?"

Jane nodded.

"When?"

"During the trial."

"Golino's trial?"

She nodded again, her eyes wide with fear.

"Golino was acquitted, right?" Pat asked. "What was that, about two or three years ago?"

As a journalist, Rachel had been all over that story, along with every other journalist on Long Island. In all fairness, though, most people would probably not have had her level of interest, especially with Ben Harrison as the lead detective on the case against the crime boss. But still, how could Pat not remember what had happened? "Yes, he got off after several key pieces of evidence went missing, and at least one witness disappeared from police custody."

From Ben's custody. Of course, it could be her cynical nature making her think the worst, but she doubted it. If Ben was on Golino's payroll, he was lost to her. The last thing Rachel needed was a run-in with Carmine Golino. Again. She probably wouldn't have survived their last encounter, when she'd gone undercover in Golino's circle, desperate to find answers about how Rebecca died, if not for Ben's intervention.

Another thought struck fear straight through her. "Is it Golino you're afraid of? Is he the one who ordered your abduction?"

Because if that was the case, they were all in a whole lot more trouble than she'd realized. And considering what they'd already been through, that was hard to fathom.

Jane stared at her and began to tremble. "I'm not saying anything else until we find Shannon."

"Okay. All right. Let's just stay calm and think." The last thing she wanted to do was agitate Jane any further. "Do you know where to find Shannon?"

She caught her lower lip between her teeth and glanced back and forth between the two of them, then nodded.

"Will you tell us?"

She shook her head. "I'll take you to her."

"Okay, fair enough."

"But only if there's no cops."

Rachel sensed Pat about to interrupt and answered before he could say anything. "Okay, fine. For now, I'll agree to that."

When Pat started to open his mouth, Rachel shot him a warning glare and hoped he understood. This girl was in trouble. Very serious trouble, and she was about thirty seconds away from taking off. If not for the blizzard raging outside, she'd probably already be gone.

He frowned and ran a hand over his beard. "Is it okay if I check you over? Tend to your injuries?"

Jane shook her head again, sank deeper into the blanket. "I just want to go to sleep."

Rachel couldn't blame her. If she were being honest, she'd love to escape into sleep herself, though she doubted it would come easily, if at all, now that she had a somewhat clearer picture of what they were up against.

Pat let it go and stood. "There are twin beds in the bedroom, so you two can have those. There are extra blankets in the chests at the foot of each bed."

Jane scrambled to her feet and gave Shadow one more petting before heading toward the bedroom.

For just an instant, Rachel wanted to suggest taking Shadow into the bedroom with them, thinking they'd both probably feel safer, but it was better for him to stay with Pat in the living room. Pat knew the big dog better, would probably realize right away if he was acting strangely or warning of anyone approaching.

"Jane, wait." Pat held out one of the hurricane lamps to her. "Here, take this."

She took it and started to turn, then looked back at both of them. "Thank you."

Rachel choked up and nodded.

Pat smiled. "Sleep well."

Once Jane had gone into the bedroom, Rachel returned to the table. As scared as she was that Pat might abandon them once he knew the truth, she couldn't let him walk blindly into this situation. It wouldn't be fair to him. He had to know what he was up against, and if he wanted to take a hike after that, well, she really couldn't even blame him. "How much do you know about Carmine Golino?"

Pat sat next to her, leaned forward and clasped his hands on the table. He pitched his voice low enough that Jane shouldn't hear him. "Reputed crime boss, arrested a few years back for a whole list of things, um…money laundering, loan-sharking, fraud, drug trafficking."

"And that was just the beginning. There were rumors of human trafficking too, though he was never charged. He's bad news, Pat, really bad news."

"So, why not go to the police?"

"Let's just say Golino has friends in high places. If we hand Jane over to the police, there's a good chance she'll disappear just like the witness during his trial did."

He propped his elbows on the table, shoved his fingers into his hair and squeezed. After a moment, he scrubbed his hands over his eyes, then let them fall to his sides. "So, now what?"

"If you want to get out of here, I'll understand." Though she prayed he wouldn't. "Leave us one of the ATVs, and you take Shadow and go while you still have the cover of darkness."

He stared at her, and his expression hardened. "Do you really think I'd leave the two of you alone and in trouble? What kind of man do you take me for?"

Rachel smiled. She couldn't help herself. If the cold, hard determination in those baby blues was any indication, he wasn't going to dump them off and head for the hills. "Well, I'm kind of hoping you won't, but in all seriousness, I would understand if you wanted to wash your hands of the whole situation. Not that I knew what I was getting into when I set out to look for Jane—to be honest, I wasn't really sure I'd find anything at all—but either way, I still made the choice to go looking for her. You didn't have that option. We just barreled through your door with gunmen on our heels. And that's not fair."

"Fair or not, it's done now." He blew out a breath, glanced at the partially opened bedroom door and leaned closer to Rachel. "Listen, when I thought there were only four men to deal with, and maybe the possibility of your cousin calling in a few more, I believed waiting here was the best option. But now, with the possibility a man with Carmine Golino's resources is involved, we can't stay put."

She jerked back, caught off guard by the idea of heading back out into the storm. But even as she rapidly weighed their options, she disagreed. The thought of getting back onto that ATV with her visor clouded and coated in ice brought momentary panic. "Between the darkness and the limited visibility brought on by the storm, I don't see how we can get out of here safely."

"That's why we're not going to take the ATVs."

"We can't very well walk out of here." Okay, while she was glad Mr. Tall, Blond and Compassionate wasn't going to dump them in the middle of the wilderness, probably, the downside was he got to have a say in how they proceeded. A situation Rachel wasn't at all used to. Experience had taught her she could only depend on herself. When Rebecca had disappeared, she'd trusted her parents, trusted the police, believed everyone would do everything in their power to find her sister and bring her home. But as the months wore on and the detectives turned to new and more urgent matters, and her parents lost themselves in a well of depression… And Ben. Even

Ben had betrayed her and given up in the end. Well, life had taught Rachel hard lessons.

She reached deep for diplomacy. "It's pitch black, there's basically a wall of snow, and we have no idea the extent of Jane's injuries since she refuses to let you examine her."

"All the more reason to get out of here." He stood, went to the door to retrieve his still wet boots then returned to the table.

"How can you even suggest running now? Why did we even bother disguising our entry into the cabin just to turn around and leave a trail in whatever direction we head? We may as well post a billboard saying, 'They went thataway.'"

Pat just grinned, and those deep blue eyes lit with mischief she might have found endearing under other circumstances. Now, however, she only found him infuriating. She flung her arm toward the bedroom doorway and tried desperately to hold on to patience. "We just sent Jane to get some sleep, and now you want to get her up and take her on the run again?"

"No." He slid his feet into the boots, winced then started on the still-stiff-with-crusted-snow laces. "You'll stay with her while I go find a vehicle to get us out of here."

"Oh, I will, will I?" So now he was issuing orders? He sounded just like her parents had all those years ago. *There, there, honey. You just go on to bed and don't worry about a thing. Rebecca got mixed up with the wrong crowd. I'm sure she'll come home when she realizes the error of her ways. You should learn a lesson from this and always do as you're told.* She lifted one brow and shot him her most scathing look.

His charming smile only intensified. "It'll be okay, Rachel. I won't be gone long, and I'll leave Shadow with you."

While that thought brought some measure of comfort since it meant he'd surely return, it did nothing to lessen her anger, some of which was surely directed toward the past, at her parents for assuming Rebecca had run away and not doing more to find her. Knowing that didn't help.

She jumped to her feet, propped her hands on her hips. "What gives you the right to just barge in and take over?"

"The two women who burst through my door in the middle of the night desperate for help. And you're going to get that help whether you like it or not. Now." With his boots on and laced, he stood and looked directly into her eyes. He lifted a hand, reached toward her and tucked her hair behind her ear, cradled her face for a moment. "There's a neighborhood not far from here. I'll grab the first SUV I come to and get right back here."

"What do you mean grab? How will you even get it started?"

"I'll hot-wire it. Don't worry. I'll explain it to the police when we finally get that far, return it and apologize. Hopefully, the owner will understand."

"Why not just knock on the door and ask to use it?"

He laughed out loud.

Laughed? Seriously? Her blood boiled.

"Better to ask for forgiveness than permission, right?

Besides, it's the middle of the night. The first thing someone will do if I knock on a door is most likely call the police."

Okay, she had to concede that one.

"Don't worry. I won't be gone long. But give me the handgun, and I'll leave the shotgun with you."

She started to argue, then just gave up and handed over the weapon.

He stuck it in his pocket, then crouched in front of Shadow, met his gaze, and some sort of silent communication seemed to pass between the two before he patted the big dog's head and stood. "Stay, Shadow."

"How do you even know how to hot-wire a car?" *Really, Rachel, that's the best you can come up with?* She massaged her temples where a dull throb had settled.

"I learned when I was a teenager and wanted to 'borrow' my uncle's Mustang for a date, and he said no. That did not end well for me." His laughter followed him out the door into the storm.

As she closed the door and locked it behind him, his question from earlier—the one she'd avoided answering—popped into her mind.

What kind of man do you take me for?

She fell back against the door, the cabin seeming even colder with his exit. *The kind of man who'd risk his life to try to save two complete strangers. The kind of man even the most jaded cynic would be tempted to trust.* "The kind of man I should steer real clear of."

After waiting for Rachel to engage the lock behind him and second-guessing his decision a hundred or so times, Pat jogged through snow past his ankles, some of the deeper drifts sucking him in up to his knees. He had to get some kind of vehicle and get them out of there before the roads became completely impassable, even with a four-wheel-drive. A rural area like the one they were in, mostly summer homes and only a small population of locals, would be the last to see a plow, and then not until at least the next day for sure. While that could work in their favor, since it meant Harrison and his men couldn't get to them, it would also put them at greater risk. At worst, with no means of escape, they'd be sitting ducks.

Despite the ticktock of the invisible clock in his head urging him to move faster, he took the time to brush away any sign of his passing with the same branch he'd used earlier. No sense giving anyone reason to check the cabins. When he reached the ATV, he jumped on and peeled out amid a blast of muddy snow shooting up from beneath the tires.

Avoiding the roadways, he kept to the woods, dodging trees and brush as he plowed on way too fast for the current conditions. As he neared the main street, bright lights penetrated the squall. A plow after all? He couldn't be sure. Not that he wanted to wait even an extra second as fear for Rachel and Jane weighed him down, but he had to be sure. He stopped in the shadow of the tree line, doused the ATV's headlight and held his breath as he waited. Though he worried the plume of exhaust might be visible from the road, no way was he turning the machine off. Besides, hopefully, the storm would act as cover.

He ducked his head low, watched the lights moving toward him on the street. As they came closer, their lights pushed back the storm enough for him to make out two dark shapes creeping down the street. Not plows, but dark-colored SUVs all but shrouded in the darkness. He held his breath. Golino's men? More than likely. Who else would be out on a night like this?

And if they were in the area, it meant they suspected Rachel and Jane had holed up nearby. He contemplated his next move: make a run for it and snag a vehicle as soon as the two rounded the next curve, or go back and protect Rachel and Jane? He shouldn't have left them alone, should have loaded up the ATVs and taken them with him. But Jane had needed rest, needed to get warm, needed to feel safe, even if only for a moment or two. And even if that safety was only an illusion.

Leaving his headlight off, since the streetlights were bright enough for him to navigate if he stayed close to the road, he started forward the instant the two vehicles turned out of sight. The snow also helped, the dark silhouettes of trees standing out in stark contrast against the blanket of white. Now if the constant barrage of snow pellets would just abate long enough for him to find help, he'd be set. He took a deep breath, bearing in mind the same blizzard that was hindering his vision was also providing the cover he needed to move stealthily and hopefully was protecting Rachel and Jane from discovery.

He struggled to lift his visor, which had fogged over as it crusted with snow and ice, hoping to gain better visibility. A sense of urgency beat at him as he followed the tree line along the road toward civilization. This was taking too long. Whatever Jane had witnessed of Carmine Golino had him worried. Terrified, if he was being straight with himself. Even if he hadn't followed the trial all that closely, he knew of the crime boss, as did most Long Islanders. It was rumored his neighborhood, which sat about an hour west of Seaport, was one of the safest on the island, as long as you stayed in Golino's good graces. It was also rumored if you fell from his favor, you ended up buried in his dumping grounds amid the Pine Barrens out on eastern Long Island, where more than one of his suspected victims had been unearthed.

Pat couldn't help but wonder how Jane had managed to cross paths with him, though he didn't blame her for this mess. As a young homeless girl, she had probably only done whatever she had to in order to survive, much as he himself had done tonight, breaking into a house and now looking for a car to hot-wire. But Rachel's cousin, Detective Ben Harrison? How could he have gotten involved with the gangster? Pat had noticed Rachel's reaction when Jane had mentioned him, the way she'd opened her mouth as if to speak, then snapped it closed just as quickly. She seemed to be warring with herself over something. Ben's involvement? Maybe, but why? Because she accepted what he'd become and resisted the initial urge to defend him? Or because she feared Jane would stop talking if she did?

Rachel. Her courage in the face of danger, her ability to see good in others—which might well prove to be a detriment no matter how refreshing he found her attitude—her commitment to helping a young girl in need, those deep green eyes with that brilliant burst of gold in their center, like a tranquil sea alight with the sun's reflection each time she smiled.

Whoa! His thoughts skidded to a stop. While he couldn't deny the hint of attraction to her beauty as well as her personality, that inner spark that made her independent and trustworthy—

Okay, enough is enough. He crouched lower, determined to keep his mind on what he was doing. Rachel was nothing more than a complication he didn't need. While he understood and accepted God's plan for him might differ from his own intentions, Rachel played a part in neither. Of that he was beyond certain. He'd watched his own parents' toxic relationship as they slowly destroyed each other for years before his mother finally couldn't take any more and, on the verge of a breakdown, walked out on his father. And him. No way would he follow in their footsteps. As an adult, he'd managed to find forgiveness for his mother, made amends and even shared a limited relationship with the woman who'd abandoned the eleven-year-old boy, but he had no intentions of ever trusting a woman so completely again, ever giving himself so wholly to another. And without that level of trust, a long-term serious relationship was out of the question.

He bumped over something in the snow, leaned heavily to the side to keep the ATV from tipping as his point was hammered home. Even thoughts of the lovely and courageous Ms. Davenport were dangerous.

A dark shape came into view across the snow-covered road. He squinted, used his hand to shield his eyes. *Yes!* The brick entryway bordering both sides of a narrow side street announced the first residential development in the area. Time to get what he needed and wash his hands of Rachel Davenport.

Pausing, he looked up and down the road, didn't see any sign of anyone in the darkness. He held his breath, listened past the pounding of his heart and the hum of the ATV's engine. Nothing but the roar of wind and ice pellets hitting his helmet.

He thumbed the throttle and lurched forward, cleared the tree line and made it almost all the way across the road when an SUV rounded the corner and pinned him in its headlights.

Countless ideas ran through his mind in a fraction of a second, and he dismissed them all. He almost lifted a hand to wave and play innocent bystander out in the storm for some fun if the men in the SUV stopped, then thought better of it. What were the chances two women and a man had fled on ATVs, and he just happened to be out riding one in the same area? Possible, but if they didn't believe him, not only was he dead, but Golino's men were that much closer to reaching Rachel and Jane.

Instead, he crouched low, hit the throttle, and bounced over the curb, across the snow-covered grass and around the brick wall. A quick glance over his shoulder told him all he needed to know as the SUV increased its speed and fishtailed around the corner onto the development's main road.

Pat flew through a backyard, skirted a brick wall surrounding the next yard and kept going. As soon as he was able, he crossed over another road and through a yard that ran into the back of the development, separated from the next property by a wide gulley. A six-foot stacked stone wall bordered the next yard, standing between it and the drainage ditch, probably to keep kids or dogs contained as much as for privacy. But a blockade between Pat and safety at the moment.

He braked, slid to a stop. Turn back? Or risk slipping down the side and overturning? He chanced a quick glance over his shoulder. Heavy wet snow gleamed and shimmered in the oncoming headlights. They'd found him. Probably not too difficult given the trail of slush he was leaving behind. Well, they couldn't follow him into the gulley with their vehicle, and he'd be able to outrun them if they abandoned the vehicle to chase him on foot. Of course, they could have radioed for another vehicle or the dirt bike riders to intercept him. But that was a problem for another time.

He had no choice; he'd have to chance it. When he hit the throttle, the ATV leapt over the edge, clung to the slope for a moment, then the tires lost their grip on the slick surface, and the machine overturned.

Disoriented, Pat pushed off to keep the ATV from landing on him and tumbled into the gulley. Pain ripped through his shoulder as he half rolled, half slid into the ditch. He landed with a splash in the frigid slushy runoff at the bottom. The cold blasted through him. He'd already lost feeling in his hands and feet, but this was different. The shock of the icy sludge stole his breath.

Ignoring the pain and the cold, he jumped to his feet before he'd even fully stopped and took off. No time to wipe his fingerprints, which Ben Harrison could easily run, from the ATV. Who knew? Maybe they wouldn't survive the storm. Pat barely spared an instant to think which way to run before heading back in the direction he'd come from. Careful to stay in the mess at the bottom, hoping the water mixed with the snow and ice would cover his tracks, he ran. God willing, his pursuers would expect him to head in the opposite direction.

Now to find a car. Of course, it wouldn't be as easy as he'd implied to Rachel to gain access. While he could hot-wire an older car, like his uncle's Mustang, newer cars had protection in place. And the chances of finding a clunker in this neighborhood, where residents could afford walls and security gates to guard their million-dollar homes, were slim to none. Even if any of the residents did own an older model car, it would most likely be a collectible kept in a garage to protect it from nights such as this and thieves such as him. He'd hoped to come across some middle-class homes amid the luxury, knew there were locals in the neighborhood, many of whom worked for the owners of the mansions dotting the area.

Rachel's suggestion to knock on a door and ask for help flitted through his mind. He dismissed it just as quickly. Even if he would risk the resident calling the police, no way could he thrust this mess upon an unsuspecting civilian.

Instead, he followed the gulley to the end of the development, scrambled up the slippery incline and crossed over the road. As he trudged through the deepening snow—lungs aching, shoulder throbbing, feet numb—

fear for Rachel and Jane prodded him forward. "God, please protect them. Please, help me protect them."

The cold ache deep in his bones begged him to stop, to take a moment, to rest. To hesitate. No way. Never again would someone die because he hesitated. He lowered his head and plowed on, one painful step at a time as the storm battered him.

How in the world had he ended up in this situation? At this moment, he should be dozing in his recliner with Shadow snuggled beside him, warm and toasty in front of the cozy fire. Instead, he was on the verge of freezing to death in the middle of a blizzard with two women's lives dependent on him. And he realized he'd never felt more complete than he did in that moment. While recuperating at his uncle's cabin had benefited him in the beginning, it had become more of a pity party than anything else of late. Even though he found his IT work enjoyable, challenging even, it didn't hold the same sense of serving God as rescue work did. Nor did it yield the same sense of accomplishment, the reward of having saved a life. At least that was one dilemma solved.

It was time for him to stop feeling sorry for himself and return to what he was always meant to do. Provided, of course, he didn't get killed before this night was through. He shoved the thought aside. He'd get through the night. And he'd get to Rachel and Jane. He had to.

Because the thought of failing them was too much to bear.

When the first hint of light pierced the raging storm, he thought his imagination was playing tricks on him.

Still, he increased his pace. It wasn't long before the silhouette of buildings came into view, and he realized he'd come to Main Street. "Oh, Lord, thank you."

He came up behind a row of shops with apartments above them and small parking lots behind, the exact kind of neighborhood he needed. He'd be much more likely to find an older vehicle amid the sporadic scattering of cars there. On his sixth try, barely clinging to hope and with his legs on the verge of giving out, he found a battered older-model Honda Civic in an alleyway between two shops. Knowing locals in small towns often left their vehicles unlocked, he yanked the driver's side door handle.

Snow spilled from the roof into the car as the door opened. *Yes!* Pat flipped down the visor. No key. He checked under the mat. Nothing. He slid inside and eased the door closed, not sure his frozen fingers would cooperate if he tried to expose the wires, then opened the glove box. The breath shot from his lungs when he found a set of keys. Now he just had to hope the owner didn't notice the vehicle missing and report it to the police before he could get back to Rachel and Jane and get them out of there. Hopefully, the storm and the late hour would keep the owner inside.

The car turned over easily, and, leaving the lights off, he crept to the edge of the alleyway, looked out and saw no one, then eased the vehicle onto Main Street. While he'd have preferred a more discreet route along back roads, he didn't know the area well enough. The compact car slid, and he had to ease off the accelerator to keep it on the road. Thousands of needles stabbed his hands and feet as the heat chased away the numbness. Ignoring the pain, he headed back toward the cabins, praying he wouldn't be too late.

FIVE

Rachel paced from one end of the cabin's main room to the other. Hugging herself, she rubbed her hands up and down her arms to chase away a chill that came just as much from inside her as it did from the cabin's cold, damp interior. Shadow had paced with her for a while but had given up and now lay on the floor in front of the door, head tilted, gaze glued to her as she moved back and forth.

"Sorry, boy." She paused, crouched to cup his massive head between her hands and ruffled his fur. "I know I'm probably making you more agitated, but I can't seem to stay still."

He leaned his head into her hand and licked her arm.

With one last pet, and the promise to herself she'd go to the shelter for a dog as soon as this was over, she stood and stretched her back, stiff from cold and probably tension. Quietly, so as not to wake Jane, she eased the bedroom door open to check on the girl, again. Still asleep, though fitfully, tossing, turning, mumbling in her sleep, she'd tangled herself in the blankets and lay exposed to the cold. Rachel had tried to make sense of the muttered words earlier but had given up when she couldn't understand anything.

Not wanting to disturb her, Rachel lifted a blanket from the second bed and laid it over her gently, then closed the door and resumed her route through the room. Pat should have been back by now. It was taking too long. What if something had happened to him? What if Golino and his men had found him? Would Ben kill Pat for helping her? She dismissed the thought, didn't have the strength to think about it at the moment. It was bad enough to have to think of her cousin as a killer. Would she ever be able to forgive him if he killed a man who'd only tried to help her and a frightened young girl? How could she?

Yet, she'd forgiven him when he'd failed Rebecca, had felt sorry for him even when he'd joined a group—gang, really—of kids who everyone knew worked for Golino. When Rebecca had gone missing, Rachel had been so sure something bad had happened to her, but no one would listen. Her parents thought she'd run away, and the police treated her like a runaway. Only Ben had listened to Rachel's increasingly desperate warnings. At first. But then, even he turned his back on her, reneged on his promise to find Rebecca no matter what it took. He decided she had probably just gotten mixed up with a bad group of kids and taken off. And hadn't Ben essentially done the same? Hooked up with Golino and his gang, retreated from everyone and everything he'd once claimed to love? He may not have disappeared physically—they knew where he was, they just couldn't reach him—but emotionally he'd completely withdrawn, may as well have been a million miles away.

The frigid air, or the chill within her, grew even colder, if that was possible. She yanked the blanket from the back of the chair and wrapped it around herself as wind howled and windows rattled beneath its force. And then another sound intruded.

Shadow lifted his head higher, scrambled to his feet, turned toward the door.

The sound grew louder, until there was no mistaking the sound of an engine or the crunch of tires against the icy snow just outside the cabin door. Hands shaking, she grabbed the shotgun off the table.

Shadow growled, crouched with his front legs spread wide. He barked once, then tilted his head to listen.

She had to get Jane up, but then what? Out the window? Or stand and fight. Jane had no weapon. Rachel grabbed the poker from the rack of tools beside the fireplace, shoved the bedroom door open with her foot and stopped, frozen in the doorway.

Other than the tangle of blankets hanging over the bed's edge onto the floor, the bed was empty.

Shadow barked, again and again.

Rachel bent and looked under the beds. Nothing. Where could the girl have gone? Rachel had been pacing outside the bedroom door on constant patrol since Pat had left. Without much hope, she shoved open the bathroom door and flipped on the light switch before remembering the power was out. She grabbed the lantern from the table, juggled it with the poker she was reluctant to put down and lifted it in the doorway. She checked behind the shower curtain. Empty.

Shadow stopped barking and whimpered. The click of his nails against the hardwood floors as he paced back and forth in front of the door masked any other sound.

Rachel ran back to the bedroom, stood in its center, turned in a circle. Nowhere to hide. Wind rattled the partially open window, nudged her with its icy fingers. Trying to listen past Shadow, she eased the window open farther to see the footprints leading away from the cabin. Only one set. "Are you kidding me right now?"

Fear for Jane's safety replaced the flash of anger almost instantly. The girl had been terrified, had no experience trusting adults, or probably anyone for that matter. She was used to depending solely on herself. Or maybe Shannon, since the two seemed pretty tight.

Okay, out the window and follow her?

Shadow barked again.

Someone pounded against the door. Jane? Pat? Surely the bad guys wouldn't knock. Leaving one lantern in the bathroom and the other in the bedroom, Rachel pulled the door shut behind her, pitching the room into darkness. No sense making a target of herself.

The pounding came again.

She peered out a gap between the shutters covering the fogged-over window. The glass was too hazy to make out anything other than a dark shape on the porch and a small vehicle beyond it.

"Rachel." The pounding again.

Pat?

She reached for the doorknob with the hand firmly gripping the poker, her gun aimed steadily at the door. Despite the cold, sweat soaked her palms, and she wished for even a moment to wipe them dry. Instead, she blew out a breath, unlocked the door and whipped it open, then braced herself to fight.

Pat held his hands out to the sides. "Just me."

Shadow ran to him, tail wagging.

"Good boy." After a quick pet, he stood and looked over his shoulder. "Come on. I've got a car, but Golino's men are all over the place. Get Jane and let's get out of here."

Rachel handed the shotgun to Pat and used the back of her hand to wipe the sweat from her brow, which had begun to freeze with the door open. "Yeah, well, that's going to be a problem."

He frowned as he stepped into the cabin, shut the door behind him. "What are you talking about?"

She turned and hurried back to the bedroom, tossed the fireplace poker onto the bed and gestured toward the window she'd left partially open. "She's gone."

"What?" He opened the window farther, leaned out, spotted the prints. "How long?"

"It couldn't be long. I'd just checked on her, covered her since she'd thrown off most of the blankets. Then, when I heard you outside, I grabbed the poker so she wouldn't be defenseless and went to get her. She was gone."

"She can't have gone far." He shoved her weapon into her hand, lifted the lantern, went into the other room then quickly buckled Shadow's harness into place.

"She'll be easy enough to track in the snow. As long as we move faster than her, we should be able to catch up. Grab her blanket."

Rachel did as he said, then swung a leg over the low window ledge, dropped and crouched in the snow.

"Wait right there, I want to move the car."

With her back against the cabin, the blanket and handgun clutched against her chest, she surveyed the area. No sign of movement. No other tracks besides those Jane had left when she'd fled. She scanned the tree line, searched every shadow for any sign they'd been found.

When she spotted movement coming toward her, she froze for an instant before catching sight of Shadow and realizing the dark blob moving quickly toward her was Pat.

As soon as he reached her, he paused and looked around, then took the blanket from her and held it out to Shadow. "Shadow, find."

Shadow lowered his head, sniffed and started forward.

When Pat began to move alongside the dog, shotgun held ready, Rachel fell into step beside him. Not knowing what to expect from the dog or how the interaction between dog and handler worked, she hung back just a little so as not to interfere. "He doesn't need a leash?"

Pat's head stayed on a constant swivel, seeming to watch everywhere at once while also keeping an eye on Shadow. "No, he'll be fine."

"Why have him search when her tracks are so easy to follow?"

"Just in case we lose her trail. It's better for him to be in work mode from the start." After that, he fell silent, the only sounds their harsh breathing and the crunch of their footsteps in the snow.

Was he not talking because Shadow needed quiet? Or because he didn't want to draw attention to them? Or did he blame her for losing Jane? She'd had one responsibility—keep the girl safe until he returned—and she'd failed miserably, again. With her nerves completely shot, she remained quiet and followed Pat and Shadow through the woods.

Tears tracked down her cheeks, and she swiped at them with frozen fingers. If they could so easily follow Jane, so could anyone else. Of course, Pat and Rachel had the advantage of knowing her starting point, but still… If anyone came across the trail they were following, it wouldn't be too difficult to find her. Rachel just had to pray they'd find the girl before anyone else did.

When Shadow stopped, perked up his ears, Pat held up a hand and crouched down.

Rachel crouched beside him, tried to listen past the howl of the wind, her ragged breathing, the blood rushing in her head. There.

Shadow tilted his head.

The unmistakable sound of a motor echoed through the forest, amplified by the blanket of snow. She lowered her head, strained to determine a direction. While she couldn't pinpoint where the sound was coming from, she was fairly certain it was moving away from them, getting fainter.

Pat stood and gestured for her to move with him but

kept his hand out to keep her back as he crept forward, leading the way. When he next held up his hand, he turned to face her and blew out a breath. "We have to go back, have to get to the car before we get cut off."

"No way I'm leaving that girl out here. You can go back, but I'll keep searching."

"She's gone, Rachel."

No. Her heart stopped. Panic assailed her, threatened to choke her. All she could manage was a harsh whisper on an outrush of breath. "Gone?"

"No, no." His eyes went wide and he gripped her arms. "I'm sorry, no. I mean, not gone *dead*, just gone."

She stared into his eyes, trying desperately to understand what he was talking about.

He stepped aside and gestured ahead of her to a churned-up section of snow. A set of tire tracks led away in the opposite direction. Wait, no, two sets, which crisscrossed each other as they led away from the scene. "Two dirt bikes."

He nodded, then looked over his shoulder at the mess and frowned. Surveilling his surroundings, he rushed forward, bent and reached out. He scooped a darkened section of snow into his hand, lifted it to his nose, sniffed. "Blood."

Rachel barely resisted the urge to scream. Jane might be gone for now, though she'd never stop searching for her, but Pat and Shadow were there, and she still held the responsibility for dragging them into this. She didn't dare do anything that might put them in any more danger than they were already in.

Pat gripped her arm. "Rachel."

Startled from her thoughts, she looked at him. "Huh?"

"I said we have to go. Now." He turned her, prodded her ahead of him, kept his shotgun at the ready.

She held out her own weapon, careful not to trip over anything buried beneath the snow as she increased her pace, navigating cautiously through the woods with only her phone's flashlight, which she should probably turn off to save the battery, but she didn't think she'd be able to find her way out of there without it.

Though she'd lost track of how long they'd been walking, it seemed like hours. They had to be close to the cabins. She sucked in a deep breath, coughed when it froze her lungs. It was time to reassess, take a moment to figure out where to go from there. At least now they had a vehicle and could get out of there. But where to go? To the police? She was still reluctant to contact them, considering Ben's involvement. She glanced at the phone in her hand. Still no service. But, if not the police, who would she call?

Shannon. If she could get back in touch with her, maybe she'd have some idea where they might take Jane. Rachel had to hold on to hope they hadn't killed her. If she was valuable enough that they'd gone through so much trouble to locate her, they'd probably kept her alive. An image of Pat holding the scoop of blood-spattered snow intruded on her thoughts. She shoved it aside. She wouldn't even consider the fact Jane could be dead. And she wouldn't stop looking for her.

"Stop," Pat hissed as he grabbed her arm and pulled her down. "Shh."

Rachel ducked behind a bush. At least the snow cov-

ering its bare branches offered some semblance of cover.
From where she knelt, she could see the silhouettes of
the cabins through the blizzard. She turned off her flashlight.

A car door slammed. Men's voices carried to her on
the wind, though she couldn't make out what they were
saying. Then a hush fell over them. She glanced at Pat.

He put a finger to his lips.

Seriously? Like she'd really talk right now. She
couldn't help the eye roll that pretty much happened
on its own before she could stop it.

Pat grinned.

And in that instant, with snowflakes and ice crys-
tals swirling around them, catching in his wet hair and
dark lashes, everything else fell away. Her fear abated.
It was as if only the two of them existed, protected by
a wall of whirling snow. She lifted her hand. Her fingers trembled as she started to reach for him, if only
to have the comfort of her hand against his cheek for
one instant, just one single moment to steady herself.

Then the world exploded.

Pat dove, trying to cover Rachel and Shadow, man-
aging about half of each. That's what he got for losing
himself in those dangerous green eyes for even a moment. Golino's men had firebombed the cabin, and he'd
been too distracted to see it coming. With Jane gone,
there was no reason to linger and chance another con-
frontation with them. Thankfully, he'd moved the car.
Now, they just had to make it to the vehicle before anyone else tracked it to where he'd parked.

He gestured through the woods. "Go."

Rachel obeyed instantly, scrambled to her feet and took off in a low crouch in the direction he'd indicated. Either she agreed with his assessment, or she'd already come to the same conclusion. Either way, he was just grateful she'd started running.

"Shadow, heel," Pat hissed quietly.

Knowing exactly what was expected of him, Shadow stayed at Pat's side as they ran.

Massive pine trees loomed in the thick stand of forest, the slap of their needled branches sharp and unforgiving, and they weaved to avoid them. The raging snow squalls seemed to be letting up, a blessing because it improved visibility. Then again, they'd be easier targets for their attackers.

"Hold up."

Rachel dropped, scanning the night for any threat.

Pat held his breath, despite the ache in his chest, and listened. No sounds of pursuit. They had to go. He kept his voice low. "Follow me. Stay close."

Abandoning caution, he sprinted for the car he'd left parked amid thorny brush. Looking back, maybe not the best idea. It had been fine when he'd cautiously emerged, but not so much in a mad dash through the pricker bushes grabbing at him to reach the vehicle. As much as he'd have liked to spare Rachel and Shadow, he didn't dare start the car until they were all inside. No telling how close Golino's men were. "The door's open."

He'd left them unlocked in case they needed to make a quick escape but had pocketed the key. He fished it out, even as he opened the hatchback for Shadow. As soon as he was inside, Pat eased the door shut gently, then gave a solid push to be sure it latched, before shoving his way through the brush to the driver's door.

Once inside, he held his breath as he turned the car on, shoved it into reverse and shot backward out of his hiding spot. A quick glance at Rachel told him she was okay for the moment, though scratches covered the backs of her hands, and a few deep ones marred her cheek and forehead. "You okay?"

"Yes." Eyes wide, teeth chattering—though whether from fear or cold, he had no idea—she snapped her seat belt. "But what about the fire? We can't leave the cabin burning."

"I can't put it out, but they have fire alarms and are connected to a service that will call for help." As he shifted into gear, he surveyed the area. No way was he going back toward the cabins or following the main road. Instead, he continued on the path toward the back of the vacation rental property. Hopefully it wasn't a dead end. Since marked fire roads traversed the area, he looked for blazes on the trees that would give him some indication of which way to go, and he breathed a sigh of relief when he spotted the first. At least he knew the road would eventually lead him back to civilization.

A quick glance in the rearview mirror showed no one following, and he chanced turning on the lights. Better to take the risk than to crash and have to run on foot again. He wished he'd thought to grab his coat, which Jane had left hanging over the back of the chair, and turned on the heater.

Rachel turned and looked over her shoulder. "You think we lost them?"

He checked the rearview mirror again, then the side mirror. "For now."

"Do you think they blew up the cabin believing we were inside?"

He'd thought about that while running, and while he wanted to hope that was the case, since it would mean they'd stop hunting them, he didn't. "I think firebombing the cabin was the easiest way to be sure to erase any evidence."

"What do you mean? What evidence?"

He adjusted the vents toward Rachel. "Any sign that Jane was there since they wouldn't want a trail for the police to follow."

"Wouldn't blowing up the cabin be more likely to bring the authorities?" She removed her boots, put her feet under the vents that had just begun to blow luke-warm air.

He kept his attention on the road, searching for markers that would show him the way to safety, or at least out of the woods. "For all they know, we could have left a note detailing Golino's involvement, Ben's involvement."

"I guess."

He averted his attention from the trail in front of him for just a moment to gauge her reaction to Ben's name. When she seemed okay, he continued. "Plus, Jane would have left fingerprints and DNA, which might be on file if she was reported missing. Why take a chance or risk the time it would take to search, when they could just torch the whole place and be done with it? Plus, there's probably a generator in one of the storage sheds some-where—easy enough to make it look like an accident."

"In the middle of a blizzard? Who would have been there?"

He shrugged. "The homeless, kids, a lost hunter—anyone who might have been seeking shelter from the storm. And if they caught us inside, all the better."

She sat back in her seat, shifted her feet closer be-neath the warming stream of air and caught her lower lip between her teeth.

He ached to take off his own soaked boots, but he didn't dare stop. In addition to the fear of their pursu-ers catching up with them, they needed to find help before Jane disappeared for good. And they had to call the police. No matter what promise Rachel had given, they couldn't find and save this girl on their own. He only hoped Rachel agreed. But how could they do that without tipping off Detective Ben Harrison? "So, now what?"

She lifted her hands, then dropped them into her lap and lowered her gaze. "I don't know."

He remained quiet, gave her time to think as he turned onto another trail, the vehicle's back end slid-ing as he rounded the corner. The small car was no good in the snow, but there was nothing he could do about that at the moment. Since he didn't trust the Watchogue Police Department, considering Ben Har-rison worked for them and would undoubtedly have friends who'd either believe him that Rachel and Pat had done something wrong or go along even if they didn't, that left heading to his hometown of Seaport, which was half an hour away in good weather. In the current conditions in a vehicle that was not meant for heavy winter weather, who knew how long it could take? He checked his phone for service. None yet.

Rachel did the same, then turned the phone off. "I don't have much charge left."

"I know a cop I can trust, but he's in Seaport." He held his breath. When she simply stared at the black phone screen clutched in her hands and chewed on her lower lip, he pushed. "He's a good man. He helped a friend of mine when she was in trouble. We don't have to give him any names, but we could get in touch, see if he can give us any advice or knows someone we could trust."

A tear dripped onto her clasped hands, and he reached out to her, covered her hands with one of his. "Hey. We'll get out of this."

"Maybe, but will it be in time to save Jane?" Leaving the phone in her lap, she used the back of one hand to wipe her tears away and turned her free hand over, weaved her fingers between his and squeezed.

He longed to wipe the tears away himself, to wrap her in his embrace and reassure her everything would be okay, but it would be a lie. He had no idea if things would work out. All he did know was he wouldn't leave Rachel or Jane in trouble. Whatever the outcome, he'd see it through, do what he could to help them. And then he'd walk away. Maybe he'd leave Seaport, go somewhere new, maybe somewhere he could make a living doing rescue work, give up the IT stuff, even though he enjoyed it and was good at it. Sitting behind a computer all day just didn't give him the same sense of purpose as rescue work. Unfortunately, since Seaport only had a volunteer fire department, he couldn't earn a living there. "I think the best—"

A loud rumble cut him short.

Lights shone through the woods.

Rachel sat up straighter, squinted to see through the windshield. "What is that?"

Relief rushed through him when he realized where they were. "It's a plow. We're running parallel to the highway." Albeit in the wrong direction. "We should come to a road in a few minutes that will take us to the highway."

She gripped his hand tighter, twisted to look out the back window. "Do you think they'll be waiting there for us?"

He only gave it a moment's thought. "Golino would have to have an army of men out to cover every road leading out of the Pine Barrens. I think we'll be fine."

"But where will we go?"

"Seaport Fire and Rescue." The name popped out with no thought at all. With it came the realization that, while he had issues trusting women, sometimes even friends, his faith in his fellow firefighters was unshakeable. Something he'd do well to consider before deciding to leave. "I have friends there who will help us. We can ditch the car at the train station, and I'll call Gabe and tell him where to find it."

"Gabe?"

"The police officer I was telling you about."

She nodded but didn't say anything.

Taking her silence for acceptance, he pushed. "Since I'm calling Gabe anyway, how do you feel about talking to him about the situation with Jane?"

She sucked in a deep shaky breath and let it out slowly, then frowned as she slid her feet back into her boots without looking at him.

He figured she wasn't going to answer. That was okay. As long as she didn't say no, he'd move ahead with the plan to confide in Gabe. And if she did try to fight him on it, he had already rehearsed an argument in favor of asking for help.

When she finally did speak, it was so quiet that he had to strain to listen past the crunch of tires against the snow and buried brush. "When my sister was only sixteen years old, and I barely fourteen, Rebecca and my parents had a terrible fight, after which Rebecca disappeared. One of the things they'd argued about was the new group of friends she was hanging out with. Trouble, they'd said. And when she went missing, they figured she ran away. They called the police, who went through the motions, but they didn't believe anything bad had happened to her. Who knows, maybe they couldn't bear the thought of it. Anyway, I tried to tell the police she wouldn't have left, tried to tell my parents. No one would listen. And they gave up. All of them gave up. Even Ben, though he held on longer than the others. In my mind, I talked to my sister every night, promised her I'd find her, help bring her home."

She lay her head back against the seat, closed her

eyes as if that would make the telling easier, or perhaps she was reliving that moment. "I failed her."

The pain and heartache in her voice, the certainty this story had a tragic ending, brought an ache to his own heart, and he once again reached for her hand, intertwined his fingers with hers, taking as much comfort as he offered.

She paused, turned her head to watch the miles pass.

He waited her out, content to feel the weight of her hand in his, knowing the telling would be easier if she did it in her own time, on her own terms. He had a strong suspicion it wasn't a story she shared often.

"By the time my parents and the police finally decided that Rebecca hadn't run away, her trail had gone cold, and she was lost to us." She looked at him then, pain radiating from her. "Until the following winter, on a night much like this one, with a blizzard threatening Long Island, when the police showed up at our door and confirmed my worst fear—Rebecca's body had been found. She'd been killed soon after she'd disappeared. And since that night, I have shouldered the guilt of not being able to find her, not being able to convince anyone she wouldn't have run away, not even being able to find out what happened to her or who killed her. I should have tried harder, should have pushed more, gone to another police station, insisted Ben keep looking when it seemed even he had stopped after he promised me he never would. But I didn't do any of those things, and Rebecca paid the price."

Pat's heart broke for the child she'd been, the burden she'd carried. "It wasn't your fault, Rachel. You were a child."

"When Shannon made me promise tonight not to tell the police, all of those memories came rushing back, threatened to crush me, and my first instinct was that they'd fail Jane just as they'd failed Rebecca. And despite that fear, I still thought about calling them."

"But you didn't." He kept a carefully neutral tone, making sure she understood he asked from curiosity, not judgment. "Why?"

Steel hardened her eyes. "Because Shannon wouldn't give me the information without that promise, and I kept it because I believe keeping your word is important, but also because there just wasn't time. Alec had already left, and I had no idea how quickly they'd arrive at the cabin. Besides, I honestly had no idea if I'd even find the girl. In the end, considering the situation with Ben, I believe I made the right choice."

Pat stiffened, tightened his grip on her hand, organized the argument in his head.

"At that time," she continued. "But now, I don't know what else to do. I'm not sure we can save her on our own. I'm no longer a frightened child but an investigative journalist who faces danger on a regular basis. That said, going up against Shannon's boyfriend and his teenage thug accomplice was one thing. Taking on Golino's army on my own is a whole different matter."

Relieved she could see reason, Pat barely resisted the urge to lift her hand and brush his lips against her knuckles. Since he didn't want to give her the wrong impression, he settled for squeezing her hand again. "No matter what, we're in this together. You're not alone this time, Rachel, and we will find Jane."

She hesitated, then seemed to think better of what she'd been going to say. "I hope you're right, because I can't bear the thought of living with that guilt again."

SIX

Rachel stared out the window watching the snow-covered miles pass and listening to Shadow's soft snores from the hatchback. At least one of them could get some rest.

The east end of Long Island was often deserted at this time of night—she glanced at the dashboard clock. Well, early morning, really—especially in the dead of winter, but there'd usually be at least someone on the roads coming or going from work or some late-night party. She bit back a sigh and glanced at Pat.

Each streetlight they passed beneath illuminated his strong profile. She had to give him credit; despite his seemingly easygoing nature, he apparently took whatever burdens life threw at him, embraced them and did the best he could to overcome. An admirable quality in a man, and in a friend. Was that what he'd become? In a matter of hours, could he really have become a friend? Maybe *friend* was too strong a term. Ally. Yes, allies was better suited to what they'd become, and he definitely possessed qualities you'd want in an ally. But could she trust him completely?

No, she couldn't trust anyone completely. And to think she'd almost blurted out everything to him, the whole sordid story of her past interaction with Carmine Golino when she began to suspect he'd had something to do with Rebecca's death, Ben's betrayal when he'd stopped looking for Rebecca and gone to work for Golino. All of it. She'd have to be more careful around him. Seemed his easygoing way elicited a desire in her to trust him—a mistake she couldn't afford to make.

She shook off the memories of Ben, of Golino, even of Rebecca. They'd do her no good now. She might not have been able to save Rebecca, but she would save Jane.

Pat pulled into the Seaport Train Station parking lot. "We'll leave the car here. If the owner reported it stolen and Ben intercepted that information, I don't want him to find the car at the firehouse. I won't bring trouble to my friends or their families. Gabe can have someone pick it up and return it to its owner."

"You haven't called him yet."

"I haven't even checked my phone for service, but I'll take care of it as soon as we get to the firehouse." He climbed out of the car and walked around to her side. Before opening the door, he studied the lot, the street, the surrounding woods.

Rachel hopped out the instant the door opened, an uncomfortable niggle at the base of her neck making her feel exposed despite the cover of darkness and the storm.

She bundled her jacket tighter around her, the night feeling even colder after the car's warm interior. She cupped her hands, blew into them for warmth then gave up and stuffed them into her pockets as she started to walk next to Pat.

Pat opened the hatchback for Shadow, then locked the doors and pocketed the key. "Heel, Shadow."

The big dog followed at Pat's other side.

Pat pulled out his phone, checked his service and scrolled through his contacts.

"Are you calling Gabe now?" She still wasn't quite sure how she felt about involving the police at this point, but no matter how hard she racked her brain, no other options were forthcoming.

He shook his head and pressed the phone against his ear. "No, my uncle."

"Your uncle? Is he a police officer?"

He shook his head again and started to say something when his uncle picked up. "Uncle Finn, it's Pat."

It was impossible to make out anything the caller said over the howl of the wind, not that she wanted to eavesdrop on Pat's conversation, but she was curious if he'd found another way to get help. Pat pressed his free hand against his ear and hunched over to block as much of the wind as possible as he continued to take long strides through the deepening snow.

While he spoke, Rachel replayed their earlier conversation. She'd left out the part where Ben had promised he'd find Rebecca. And he'd tried, it seemed, at first. And then he got caught up with Golino's thugs, started hanging out with the young street rats that did Golino's bidding in the hopes of moving up in his organization. And he'd turned away from his family, his friends and Rachel. No matter how many times she'd sought him out, he always turned her away, kindly at first, but then, after Rebecca's body was found, he'd become mean. She shivered at the memory of their last conversation, the one where she'd pleaded with him to leave Golino, begged him to come home to his family. She hadn't wanted to lose him too. She needed him, begged him to help her find whoever was responsible for Rebecca's death. And he'd slapped her. With an open hand, but it had still stung. Truthfully, it stung to this day.

She'd walked away then and had only seen him once more after that, when he'd intervened on her behalf with Golino, until tonight. Or last night, she supposed.

Tucking the phone back into his pocket, Pat laid a hand on Shadow's head while they walked, and she found herself wishing he'd have intertwined his fingers with hers instead. "Sorry about that. I had to call and warn my uncle."

Shaking off the ridiculous thought—blaming sheer exhaustion and nerves to excuse the momentary lapse—Rachel tried to refocus. "Warn him?"

He studied her, snowflakes catching and melting in his lashes as he blinked them away, cheeks red and raw from the cold. "I don't want Golino's men going after him."

She stopped short, the rest of the world falling away as her full attention riveted on him. "Why would anyone go after your uncle? Golino and his men don't even know who you are or that you have any involvement in this."

"The cabin I was staying at belongs to my uncle. How long do you think it will take Detective Ben Harrison to put two and two together, especially if he gets there soon enough to lift my prints from the ATV before the storm can erase them, and figures out the only occupied cabin around for miles belongs to my uncle?"

All the breath whooshed from her lungs. She was fully aware of the risks Pat was taking to help them, but she hadn't considered how it might affect his family, and she should have. "I am so sorry, Pat. I never meant to bring this on you."

"Hey." Using one ice-cold finger, he swiped away a tear that rolled down her cheek, then held her upper arms in his strong grip. "This is not your fault. Do you understand me? Jane needed help, and I truly believe God guided you both to me."

Did she believe that? Possibly. She had prayed for help, had begged God to intervene and help her save Jane, so how could she then question Pat's involvement when he'd been the answer she'd sought?

"Besides." He grinned then, and for the first time she noticed the dimple beneath his beard. "This was just the boot in the duff I needed to get me to stop feeling sorry for myself and start living again. So, enough of that. Let's go."

"Will your uncle be okay?"

"He'll be fine. He spends his winters in Florida right now, and he's going to pack up and go stay with a friend for a few days. No one will find him." He laughed out loud then. "Finnegan Ryan, one of the finest and toughest Irishmen I ever did meet, is now a snowbird. Who'd have ever thought?"

Rachel laughed. "That's quite the Irish brogue."

"Indeed it is. Not that I've ever been to Ireland, but me Uncle Finn came from there as a wee boy and never did lose the heavy accent."

"I'd love to meet him one of these days." She caught herself as she finished the sentence. Lost in a joyful moment with him, she'd forgotten about their circumstances. "I mean, uh… He sounds like a real character."

"Aye, lass, that he is. And I'd love for you to meet him. I think you'd really like him, and I know he'd like you." His gaze lingered on hers for a moment longer than necessary.

She shifted her eyes away first. While she understood the dangerous circumstances that had thrown them together and the fact that they had been forced to depend on each other for survival had most likely heightened their emotions and their feelings toward each other, it seemed Pat Ryan was wriggling his way into her heart. It was definitely time to take a step back. If she didn't, she could end up trusting this man, believing in him and being left with her heart shattered when he ultimately betrayed her. No way would she live through that again. Better to keep her distance.

When he stuck his hands into his sweatshirt pockets, she did the same and walked beside him. "Thank you, Pat. It felt good just to laugh, even if only for a moment."

He bumped her shoulder with his arm. "Anytime."

They walked in silence then, creeping through the

neighborhood as lights began to flicker on, spilling over the unmarred snow in cozy invitation. There'd be a snow day for sure, closing all the schools and probably a good portion of the businesses, but people would still have to get up—some for work, others to care for children, some just because they rose early despite having nowhere to go.

"You doing okay?"

His voice startled her and she jumped. "Huh? Yes."

"We're almost there. Through two more yards and we'll come out on Main Street behind my friend's flower shop. From there, the firehouse is right across the street."

She nodded and sank deeper into the too-thin jacket.

With a destination near, Pat picked up the pace.

"Why haven't you called Gabe yet?"

"Your phone's already dead, and mine will be soon. I want to save it in case we have to run again and need the flashlight."

And yet, he'd used what little he might have had left to call and warn his uncle. Her admiration for him grew.

"I'll be able to borrow a couple of chargers at the station and call from there."

"How long have you lived in Seaport?"

"Born and raised here."

She looked around at the small beach town, similar to so many others dotting Long Island, and imagined Pat as a child, running the streets with his friends, then going home to a house filled with love. "You must have been happy growing up here."

He shrugged. "My mother left when I was eleven."

"I'm sorry."

"Don't be. Plenty of kids had it worse. Besides, before she left, all she and my father did was fight. They were—" he hesitated and frowned "—like poison to each other, if that makes sense. Individually, they did okay, but put them together and the relationship was toxic."

"Do they still live here?"

"Nah, my mother took off and never looked back. She's still on Long Island but farther in. My father remarried a few years after she left. He moved to Texas when I was fifteen."

"Ouch, that must have been rough. You didn't want to go with him?"

"I'd just started high school, had been with the same friends since preschool, and I preferred their company to my father's." He shrugged as if it didn't matter, but the pain etched in his features as he averted his gaze belied the casual dismissal. "If I'm being completely honest, it was mostly a relief. My father was an abusive man, and I don't really blame my mother for leaving him, though I wish she'd taken me with her. Anyway, I moved in with Uncle Finn, who I'd already spent most of my time with anyway. He was more of a father to me than my old man ever was."

Rather than push the issue, she let it drop. She understood past pain, understood wanting to keep certain parts of yourself closed off more than most people could. "And when did you get Shadow?"

At the mention of his name, Shadow looked toward her, and she longed to reach out and weave her fingers into his fur.

"Three years ago. At first, I just wanted the company, but when we started obedience training, Shadow did really well. I'd taken a training course one time that mentioned search and rescue dogs and tracking dogs and thought the training might be good for Shadow. Tracking turned out to be his thing, and he just took to it, really enjoyed the classes and then later the work." When he looked down at his faithful companion, love shone in his eyes.

For just an instant, a spark of envy tried to surface. He seemed to have a bond with his dog that she didn't have with most people. Rachel tamped the thought down. She'd been the one to pull away, to distance herself from those around her after Rebecca was killed. Though she'd needed the space at the time, maybe closing herself off from everyone hadn't been the best idea.

While she'd viewed her parents' withdrawal into themselves when she'd needed them—first to find Rebecca and then to comfort Rachel in her grief—as a betrayal, perhaps the truth was more complicated than that. She'd been so burdened by the grief she'd shouldered, she'd never given much thought to how her parents must have felt, the guilt they must have carried for believing Rebecca had just run off, for not looking for her sooner, harder. Who knew? Maybe Ben had suffered his own share of guilt as well.

But because of the pain and trauma she'd suffered, Rachel hadn't been able to maintain friendships in high school. She'd kept to herself, had drifted through the years alone, alienated from everyone. Even her career choice had her spending most of her time distanced from others. While she might have to interact with people, she didn't have to allow them into her heart.

It might have been nice to have a dog, though difficult considering she often had to travel for work. But still...the thought appealed to her. Being close to another person though—trusting someone enough to let them in—well, that was a different story.

"What about you? Do you live around here?"

"About a half hour farther west." Not too far that she wouldn't be able to see him again if they survived this nightmare. As friends, of course. She might not be ready, ever, to commit to a relationship, but they'd been through so much together already. Well, she'd be lying to herself if she didn't admit to wanting to get to know him better, wanting to become friends and even wanting to meet his Uncle Finn.

"There's the firehouse." He gestured ahead of them to where light spilled out onto the snow in welcome.

"Was your uncle a firefighter?"

This time the grin lit his eyes. "Indeed he was, and right proud when I followed in his footsteps."

She couldn't help but smile back at him, even as her teeth began to chatter.

"Come on." With a quick glance up and down Main Street, Pat grabbed her hand and bolted for the front door. He looked around again as he held the door open and ushered her and Shadow inside.

The first thing to hit her was the delicious aroma of breakfast cooking, the scent as welcoming as the lights had been. Her stomach growled. She hadn't yet eaten dinner when Shannon had called her the night before, and she was starving.

As she unzipped her coat, Pat led her through a short hallway to a large room holding a scattering of tables. Couches and armchairs created a separate seating area with a large TV on the wall, currently tuned to the weather report.

A giant of a man, the overhead light reflecting from his bald head, stood and held out a hand the size of a baseball mitt. "Pat, it's great to see you up and around again, man."

"Big Earl, how are you?" Pat offered his hand.

The name Big Earl sounded familiar, and it only took Rachel a moment to place him as one of the firefighters who'd been injured in a condo fire when a floor had collapsed. She'd been out of town when the fire had taken place, but she'd read about it afterward. Although three firefighters had been injured, they'd all survived.

As Big Earl shook Pat's hand, he pulled him into a one-armed embrace, patted his back. "I'm doing okay. Now, if I could just get Serena to stop doting."

"So, let me get this straight. Your wife dotes on you, and you're complaining about that?"

"I know. I'm a fool, right? But what can I say?" He laughed, a deep booming sound. "And how are you?"

"Good, good. I'm feeling better every day."

He stood back and studied Pat as a father might a child. "Yeah?"

"Yeah, honest." Pat shrugged out of his soaked sweatshirt and hung it on the back of a chair, then took Rachel's jacket from her and did the same. "Big Earl, this is Rachel Davenport."

"The journalist?" He extended a hand, which practically swallowed Rachel's up.

"I am, yes." Touched that he recognized her name, she smiled. "It's nice to meet you."

"The pleasure's all mine. I've seen some of your work on the local news. The piece on homeless teens was especially enlightening. Good work, very good work. My wife volunteers at the hospital and always says the problem is more widespread on Long Island than people realize." He stepped back and gestured toward the table as he turned his attention to petting Shadow. "Sit, please, you're just in time for breakfast. Afraid it's nothing fancy, but Jack is making up scrambled eggs and pancakes if you're hungry."

Pat stilled, his hand resting on the chair he'd been about to pull out for Rachel. "Jack's here?"

"He is." Big Earl grabbed a towel from a cabinet against the back wall and held it out to Pat. "Now why don't you sit down and tell me what you've gotten yourselves into that has the two of you out on a night like this and looking like you're about to jump out of your skin at the slightest provocation?"

Rachel glanced back and forth between them as they eyed each other with a sort of silent communiqué passing between them, and she had no doubt if this man had children, they didn't get away with much.

"Thanks." Pat took the towel from him, then pulled out her chair and waited until she sat. While Big Earl returned to his seat and kept a careful watch on Pat, Pat dried Shadow's fur and paws and tossed the towel into a basket in the corner, then filled a bowl with water and placed it on the floor.

Once he was done, he slumped into the chair next to Rachel's. Propping his elbows on the table, he cradled his face in his hands, then sighed and shoved his hands through his hair. When he sat up straighter, hair standing up in unruly tufts, he seemed to have resolved whatever internal struggle had been waged. "I need help, man. We're in trouble, and a young girl's life is on the line."

Big Earl spread his hands. "Tell me what you need."

The tension knotting Pat's gut began to unravel. Just like that, no questions asked, his old friend was willing to help, as would all his fellow firefighters be. And the fact that Jack Moretta was there eased his anxiety even further. Jack was a friend, one who'd do anything he could and then go beyond, one he fully trusted. "For starters, I need to charge our phones, and I need to get ahold of Gabe."

"I can do that." Big Earl stood and walked out of the room.

When Pat turned to Rachel, she frowned. "Do you think we did the right thing coming here?"

Did he? He wasn't sure, couldn't ever know a hundred percent if he'd made the right choice. He lifted his hands, let them fall. "I don't know. All I know is this is where I felt most compelled to come."

She nodded and lowered her gaze.

"What?"

"I just hope we don't end up bringing trouble to your friends."

"Me too. But I don't know what else to do, where to turn." He swiveled in his chair to face her fully, gripped her trembling hands in his. "Jane needs help, Rachel. We can't trust the police just yet because of Ben's involvement, and I'm at a loss."

"You're right. I know that in my heart."

"But?"

"I guess I just got too used to handling things on my own."

"No one can go through life without depending on others." Something he'd forgotten and would do well to remember.

She frowned at him, shook her head. "How do you do that?"

"Do what?"

"Trust so easily."

Pat reluctantly released her hands. "I don't. Believe me, trusting the people here didn't come easy. It came after years of getting to know most of them, some since childhood. It came after working beside them, risking my life for them and knowing with complete certainty that they'd risk theirs for me as well. No, trust never comes easy. Not for me, anyway."

"No, me neither. But I—"

"Pat." Jack strode across the room and opened his arms in welcome. "How's everything?"

"I'm doing okay." Pat stood and hugged him, then stepped back. "And how are you and Ava doing?"

"Everything's good." He grinned and petted Shadow. "Lots of wedding plans."

"And Mischief?" Even the thought of the adorable little girl brought warmth to Pat's heart.

"Earning her nickname, that's for sure." Jack laughed, but then sobered quickly. "Big Earl told me you're in trouble. He went to hunt up a couple of chargers from the office, but he'll be right in."

"Thanks." He introduced Rachel, and Jack greeted her with a welcoming hug.

Then he held out a cell phone to Pat. "In the meantime, you can use my phone to give Gabe a call. Then why don't you sit, and we'll eat while you tell us what's going on?"

Grateful for the help without wasting time with a million questions, Pat took the phone. "Sure thing, Jack. Thanks."

"Anytime. I'll be back in a few."

"Jack's a good guy, Rachel. Try to relax for a few minutes, take advantage of the moment of peace. I have a feeling it might be a while before we get another." He laid a hand on her shoulder. "If you'll excuse me a minute, I'm going to step into the garage to call Gabe. You'll be safe with these guys until I get back."

She looked him in the eye and laid her hand over his. "I'll be fine, Pat."

He knew she would, and yet, the thought of leaving her, even though he'd only be just outside the room and his friends would be with her, brought a wave of anxiety. Was it because he was afraid Golino's men would find her? It probably wouldn't take long. Once they identified Finn as the owner of the cabin, a little research would show Finn's relationship to Pat and the fact that Pat had been injured in the line of duty. Would they figure out he'd been the one staying at the cabin? Maybe, but either way, they'd probably check the firehouse at some point since he and Finn both had a connection. Still, they should have a little time before that happened. Hopefully they'd be long gone by then.

Another concern had gotten under his skin: the fear that Rachel would take off alone in search of Ben or Golino or Jane. The way Rachel seemed to put others ahead of herself made him fear she'd ditch him and set out on her own in order to protect him. No way was that happening. He wouldn't be that easy to shake. He was in this until the end now. And then, well, he'd cross that bridge when he came to it. Walking away from the first place he'd turned to for help—the safe space he'd sought when he'd been in trouble, the friends who offered anything they could without even asking questions—might prove more difficult than he'd realized while sitting alone and isolated in that cabin in the middle of the woods contemplating where his path might lead.

Jack returned with a small stack of dishes. As he began to set the table, Pat shook off his thoughts, stepped aside and scrolled through Jack's contacts for Gabe's number.

When he found Gabe's name, he hit the number and glanced over his shoulder.

Rachel laughed as she helped Jack set out dishes with Shadow dancing along beside her, no doubt hoping someone would sneak him a piece of bacon.

Then he stepped out into the garage. Surely Jack was sharing stories of his fiancé Ava's three-year-old daughter, Missy, who was both amazing and a real handful. While Pat had always held on to the certainty he'd never get married or have a family, something about that little girl tugged at a part of him that ached for a home filled with children's laughter. Thankfully, Gabe picked up and kept him from having to examine his conflicted feelings.

"Hey, Jack. Please tell me Mischief didn't get into anything that's going to drag me out in this weather."

"Not this time." Pat laughed. "It's Pat, Gabe, I'm just calling from Jack's phone."

"Oh, whew, that's a relief."

It was also a relief to know that Gabe would have braved the blizzard in a heartbeat if something had been wrong, "Yeah, well, don't be too relieved yet. I have a problem, and I'm not sure what to do."

"What's up?"

"First, do you know a Detective Ben Harrison?"

He hesitated, just a fraction of a second, but still… "Yeah."

Since they didn't work out of the same station, he'd been hoping Gabe wouldn't know Ben. Then again, if he did, maybe he would know if Ben was dirty. "How well?"

Silence hummed for a moment that stretched on. Pat waited Gabe out. If he was friends with the man, trusted him, Pat would have to rethink his decision to ask Gabe for help.

Gabe cleared his throat. "Why are you asking?"

Trust him or not? He only had a split second to make the decision. Truthfully, he had no other options. He'd known Gabe since he was a kid. He and Gabe and Jack had all grown up in Seaport and been friends for most of their lives. Surely Pat would know if Gabe was the kind of man who could throw in with Golino. Then again, Rachel had said she and Ben were close at one time too. She'd trusted him, and she still couldn't accept the fact that he'd gone to work for Golino. "Look, Gabe, I…there's a young woman in trouble, and I'm trying to help her, but right now, I need you to be a friend first, then a cop. Can you do that?"

"Sure. For now. But if you're involved in something illegal, you know I can't look the other way, right?"

Relief lifted a weight from his shoulders. He'd gotten the exact answer he'd hoped for: Gabe would help him, but there was a line he wouldn't cross. "Thanks, Gabe, I knew I could count on you."

"Sure, man, now why don't you tell me what's going on?"

Pat ran through the story…at least, the story as he knew it, deliberately leaving out Ben Harrison's involvement. As he relayed the information to Gabe, beginning with Jane and Rachel tumbling through his door, detailing their run from their pursuers, and rehashing the conversation between him, Rachel and Jane regarding Golino's involvement, Gabe remained quiet. When Pat finished, he waited to see if Gabe would connect the dots from Golino to Harrison. It took less than three seconds.

"So, where does Ben Harrison fit in?"

Pat didn't answer immediately, not because he didn't want to pass on the information, but because he searched for a way to ask Gabe's opinion on Ben without accusing the man of being a dirty cop.

Gabe cleared his throat. "I assume he fits in somewhere. One, because you asked about him specifically and, two, because everyone suspected Harrison was involved with Golino before the trial, but once evidence and a protected witness went missing—well, it's pretty much common knowledge in the department that Ben Harrison is Golino's man. And he's not alone."

The breath rushed from Pat's lungs. He didn't know whether to feel relief or outright fear. On the one hand, at least they had confirmation about their suspicions. On the other, well, his heart ached for Rachel, because the truth would undoubtedly hurt her. Either way, he didn't have time to waste. With that in mind, he told Gabe the rest.

After listening to all of it, Gabe sighed. "Looks like I'm going to have to go out in this weather after all."

"Sorry about that, Gabe." But was he? Not really, considering they might now at least have some resources to find Jane.

"Funny, you don't sound the least bit sorry. Contrite is clearly not a good fit for you." Gabe laughed, but sobered quickly. "Give me a couple of hours to look into this and see what I can find out."

"Gabe, man…" Pat hesitated, not wanting to give the impression he wasn't grateful. But the sense of urgency battering him just wouldn't relent. "I'm not sure the girl has a couple of hours."

"All right, just sit tight until I get back to you."

"Thanks, Gabe." Pat disconnected and returned to the break room, where Rachel, Big Earl and Jack sat with a few of the other firefighters laughing over omelets and pancakes. When he reached the doorway, though, he paused.

Rachel appeared comfortable enough with his friends, seemed to fit right in actually. Shadow lay at her side as if they belonged together, chin resting on his paws. For a moment, he imagined her sitting there under different circumstances, without the pressure of a young girl's life hanging in the balance, and then she looked over her shoulder. When her gaze landed on his, her eyes filled with fear. No, this was no normal moment, no group of friends just hanging out and shooting the breeze. He'd do well to remember that and get out of there with Rachel before he brought danger to the very people he'd turned to for help or their families.

"Hey, you gonna stand there all day blocking the doorway or what?" Jaelyn Reed, a fellow firefighter and friend, punched his arm as she slid past him with a pile of clothes in hand. "Come on and eat something while your girl gets changed into something dry. Thankfully, I keep spare clothes in my locker."

"Thanks, Jaelyn." He let Jaelyn precede him, then followed her into the room, ignoring the comment about "his girl."

"Sure thing." She stopped and handed the pile to Rachel, then took a seat on one side of her.

Pat sat on her other side.

"Hey, Pat, these guys roped me into doing a DNA

test, sold it as a fun look into our history. Want in?" Jaelyn grinned and set a box on the table. "See if any deep dark secrets fall out of the Ryan family closets?"

He laughed. "Thanks, but I think I'll pass."

For now, he needed his full focus on Rachel and Jane.

While the others laughed and talked, Rachel leaned toward Pat and pitched her voice low. "Did you talk to your friend?"

"I did." Pat took a plate with a western omelet from Jack and thanked him. He hadn't even realized how hungry he was until faced with the scent of breakfast. "He said to wait for him to get back to us. He's going to see what he can find out."

She caught her lower lip between her teeth and nodded, staring absently at the pile of clothing in her hands.

"You okay?"

She glanced up at him. "If we can't do anything yet anyway, I need to go home. Only for a few minutes."

"I thought you wanted to get ahold of Shannon?"

"I tried to text her." Her fear-filled gaze met his. "She hasn't responded. I sent another message for her to call me as soon as possible."

He nodded. What could he say to ease her obvious fear for the girl? Nothing. Sometimes it was better not to say anything, so he remained silent on the subject.

"I need to stop home for my notes from the article I did on homeless teens, see if there might be a clue in there to her whereabouts. Or Jane's."

"Okay. You can use the locker room to change, then we'll go."

When she stood, thanked Jaelyn once more and excused herself to change into the dry clothes, he contemplated the wisdom of honoring her request to go home. While he understood how difficult it was to sit and do nothing, he wasn't sure returning to her house was the best idea. Assuming Ben knew where she lived, wouldn't that be the first place he'd look for her? Then again, a young girl's life was at stake, and if Rachel had information that could help find her, how could he refuse? Problem was, Rachel's safety mattered to him as well. Rachel mattered, probably a lot more than she should.

SEVEN

Rachel snuggled deeper into the heated seat of the SUV they'd borrowed from Jack, pulling the coat Pat had lent her tighter around herself, allowing his scent to cocoon her in the illusion of safety, even if only for a few brief moments. Jaelyn had been kind enough to lend her jeans, a sweater and a pair of warm socks. She'd even had a pair of warm boots that were a size too big but extremely welcome and a knit scarf. But she hadn't had a jacket, so Pat had lent her his. "You're sure Shadow will be okay at the firehouse?"

"He'll be fine. He spends a lot of time with me there, and I do leave him when we get a call and he's not needed."

She appreciated that he didn't push against her on returning to her apartment, though the fact that he'd left Shadow behind told her he didn't necessarily think it was safe to do so. "Make the next right."

What would he think of her one-bedroom apartment, more of a home base than an actual home? She'd never bothered to decorate in any traditional way, hadn't leaned toward any particular style as she'd bought, as needed, her few random pieces of furniture based on what was on sale. While she loved being a journalist, and enjoyed traveling for work at times, she hadn't yet hit it big. Ironically, the biggest story she'd ever done had been the one on homeless teens on Long Island for the local news—enough to give her some recognition locally, but still...

"Is there a code for the gate?"

She rattled it off. While decor might not have been high on her list of priorities, security was. The front gate required a code and remained locked at all times.

"I'm not going to park right in front of your unit." He crept slowly up and down rows and rows filled with cars, the apartment complex parking lot much fuller than it would normally be because of the storm. "We get in and out as fast as possible, and if anything seems off, we get out of here right away. Understand?"

Rachel bristled. Not that she disagreed with him, but it seemed Mr. Thinks He's In Charge was getting a little too used to flipping orders and expecting her to obey. "I'm not stupid, Pat."

He reached for her hand.

She slid it out of his reach.

"Hey." He stepped on the brake, waited for the car to slide to a full stop then made eye contact and held it. "I don't think you're stupid at all. I think you're courageous and kind, and maybe a bit reckless, but not at all stupid."

Not knowing whether to take that as a compliment or an insult, especially in her current mood, she shifted her gaze away from his and reached for the door handle.

"Hold on." He gripped her arm.

She glanced pointedly at his hand, lifted her gaze to meet his and raised a brow.

He released her. "I just meant there's an empty spot at the end of the next row. If you give me a sec to park, we can walk in together."

She thought about climbing out right then and there anyway just to prove a point, but Pat was right about one thing: she wasn't stupid. So, instead, she simply nodded and clasped her hands together in her lap. Though a quick scan of the parking lot—the rows of attached one-story apartments in front of and behind them and the woods at the far end of the complex—showed no sign of activity, she couldn't rid herself of the feeling something was wrong. The snow had begun to taper off, but no one was shoveling or clearing the parking lot yet.

As soon as Pat parked, she opened the door and got out, then looked around before easing the door shut as quietly as possible.

Pat turned up his collar and rounded the front of the car. When he reached Rachel, he smiled and lifted the jacket's hood over her head, propping it down low to cover part of her face. He then hooked an arm through hers and started forward. "Which unit?"

"The second from the right."

He nodded and pulled her closer. "If anything looks wrong, run."

"He probably figured I wouldn't—" *be foolish enough to* "—return home."

"Maybe." He glanced over his shoulder, then returned to looking straight ahead. "Is there a back entrance?"

"No, there's an attached apartment behind me, so only the front door and two windows, one in the bedroom and one in the living room." What had seemed like a safety feature when she'd rented the apartment, given no one could break in any other place but the front, now made her feel caged. Rachel's heart pounded, but she resisted the urge to rub her chest, tried to appear as normal as possible as they hurried up the walkway.

She clutched the key tightly in her hand, was about to stop and unlock the door, when she noticed the broken window. "Keep walking."

Outwardly, there was no indication Pat had heard the desperate whisper, but she felt his body stiffen beside her. "What's wrong?"

"The window," she hissed. And the brief view she could get inside the room sent her heart rate in to overdrive.

Pat squeezed her hand. "We have to get out of here."

"Keep walking to the apartment next door. The Brinkmans are in Pittsburgh visiting their youngest who just gave birth to their twelfth grandchild." A fact they'd talked about for weeks to anyone who would listen. She looked at him and forced a smile, which probably looked more like a grimace but would hopefully fool anyone who was watching them. "I have a key to their apartment to water their plants. We can go in there and figure out what to do."

He smiled back and nodded, and if she couldn't see the dark storm in his eyes, she'd have fallen for the casual pose as he slung an arm around her shoulders and pulled her closer.

She held her breath. Her hands shook as she shifted through the keys on her ring, then unlocked the door, waited for Pat to enter and closed the door behind them. She turned the lock and yanked her hood off. "Great. Now what?"

Pat peered through the blinds, then eased them almost all the way closed. "We have to get out of here, Rachel."

She slumped against the door, cradled her face in her ice-cold hands. He was right. They did have to get out of there, probably shouldn't have come in the first place. She wanted to scream. The thought that it would draw unwanted attention only infuriated her further. "Do you think someone's waiting inside the apartment?"

"I don't know." He crossed the room, pulled a side table away from the wall and pressed his ear against the common wall between the Brinkmans' apartment and her own. "What's on the other side of this wall?"

"My bedroom."

"Is that where your notes are?"

She nodded. "There's a file cabinet beside my desk where I keep all of my notes and a case full of flash drives beneath where my computer's supposed to be."

"What do you mean supposed to be?"

"From what I could see through the mangled blinds, my computer's gone." She shoved her hands into her hair, gripped the strands and squeezed. "What do you think the chances are some random strangers broke in and stole my computer?"

He lifted his hands to the sides, looked around the room then pressed his ear back against the wall without bothering to answer. While electronics were often taken during a burglary, what were the chances she was randomly robbed at the same time she was going up against Golino?

She inhaled deeply, counted to ten and exhaled, forcing her body to relax as she did so. She had to think, to prioritize. Most important on her list, aside from finding Jane, and somehow keeping both Pat and herself alive long enough to do so, was getting in touch with Shannon. She might be their only hope. *If* she had answers. And if she was willing to share them.

She whipped out her phone, dialed Shannon's number. No answer.

"We can't wait around here any longer." He looked back at the wall. "I can probably break through this wall, get into the bedroom."

"That would make too much noise." And the last thing they needed was to draw undue attention.

He nodded in agreement. "Probably. But the only other choice is to go in the front, and I'm not sure it's the best option. If there's someone waiting inside, or watching from somewhere close by, they could be on us before we can get out."

She had to think and needed time they didn't have.

"Only you know how important your notes are, so I'll leave the choice up to you."

She paused a moment, ran that through her head. She had begun to think he wasn't a team player, wanted to give orders and have her blindly follow, but maybe she'd read him wrong. Maybe he could follow as well. It didn't take long for her to realize she could live with that. After all, wasn't compromise a good thing?

"So, what do you think?"

His voice jarred her from thoughts she was better off not contemplating. The fact that her mind could have even wandered down that path while her world was literally falling apart around her was a problem for a later time. "Let's just go. I think I can remember some of the places from my notes. And if I can't, well, we can't save anyone if we're dead."

He slid the side table back into place and went to the front window to peer out the blinds.

"I'm sorry I insisted on coming here." She joined him, peeked out into the snow-covered parking lot. At least the snow had pretty much stopped. But was that a good thing or not? Sure, it would make it easier for them to drive, but it would also bring out a lot more people, including Golino's men. "It was a waste of time since it's not safe to go into my apartment, and it put us in unnecessary danger."

"I wouldn't say it was a waste of time."

"How do you figure?"

"Well, we know now that Ben definitely recognized you."

"I al—"

He held up a finger and interrupted before she could finish. "We suspected he did, but we couldn't be completely sure before now. And, we also know he's got men waiting for you to show up here."

"What do you mean?" She leaned closer to the window, looked through the mostly closed blinds while being careful not to get too close to the window.

"See the dark-colored SUV at the far end of the lot?"

She scanned the crowded lot, located the vehicle in question. "What makes you think that's his men?"

"It's been there since we arrived."

"So have all of the cars out there, most of which are snowed in."

"Ahh, but he's not. Aside from the fact that the SUV is cleared off, tire tracks lead through the deeper snow he's parked in, while the other cars have the snow drifted up around them. Plus, check out the tailpipe."

She did as instructed. "The snow doesn't cover it like it does on most of the parked cars."

"And if you look really close, there's smoke coming from it, which means it's running."

"So, why didn't they come in after us?"

He shrugged and stepped back. "Probably waiting to see what we do. We showed up in a borrowed car and keyed straight into this apartment, so they're probably watching and waiting to see what we do next."

Rachel shoved her hair back out of her face, at a loss as to how they'd get out of there without tipping off their pursuers. "So, what are we going to do next?"

He checked his phone. Still no word from Gabe, who'd promised to contact him the minute he learned anything. "We may be able to walk right back out of here. Ben may have given a description of you, but bundled up the way we are, we might get away with it."

Rachel didn't see it. She'd dealt with Golino before, and he was not naive. Plus, people in his employ didn't move up in rank by being outwitted. And those who didn't have the ambition to move up in rank weren't kept around for long. Golino didn't abide slackers.

"Or we could go out that way." He gestured toward the side wall. While Rachel's apartment was sandwiched between the Brinkmans and the Tyrells, the Brinkmans' unit was on an end, which meant it boasted a window on the side wall that Rachel's didn't. "If they think we're still in here, it could buy us some time to get away."

"Maybe." It could also get them killed if Golino ordered his men to firebomb the apartment before they had time to run.

She'd kind of held on to hope that Golino would just let her go, or maybe Ben would intervene on her behalf again, but clearly that wasn't the case. This time, he was probably determined to see her dead. Which meant she was going to have to tell Pat the truth—all of it. She sighed. It wasn't fair to ask him to put his life on the line without letting him know just exactly how much danger he was in. "Pat, there's something I haven't told you. About Golino. And me. And Ben."

He leaned his back against the wall, crossed one ankle over the other and folded his arms across his chest. "Yeah, I kind of got that impression."

That caught her off guard. "You knew I was leaving something out, and yet you risked your life to help me anyway?"

He shrugged in the casual, easygoing way she'd come to find endearing. "I figured you had your reasons. Plus, the fact that they took your computer and most likely the notes you returned for tells me there's something more than meets the eye going on here. So…what do you say we go with full disclosure from here on out? Okay?"

She lowered her gaze and nodded. "I'm sorry, Pat."

"Hey." He shifted away from the wall, propped a finger beneath her chin and lifted her gaze to meet his. "It's all good. But I want to help you, and I can't if I don't know all of what's going on. Fair enough?"

She nodded and felt the loss when he lowered his hand. She thought about sitting down, but she didn't want to track the mess they were leaving anywhere else in the apartment.

"I had a…run-in, I guess you'd call it, with Golino once before."

He frowned and tilted his head but remained quiet, giving her time to remember.

"It was back during Golino's trial but early on, before the evidence and witness went missing. I was working on a story." Of course, the way she'd thrown herself into her work, she'd always been working on a story, always with the hope of one day figuring out what had happened to Rebecca, of finding her killer.

Pat watched her, his gaze lingering, but she saw no judgment in his expression, only concern.

"I ran into an old friend of Rebecca's. She told me she'd heard Rebecca was employed by Golino, working his parties. Rumor had it he used young women— teenagers mostly, some runaways, some abducted, most held against their will—to work as servers, clean up after guests and…well…" Heat flared in her face, not from embarrassment but anger at a man who could take advantage of a young woman going through a difficult time. "Sold them to his friends, if you understand what I mean."

His jaw clenched and he nodded.

"So, anyway, supposedly, someone saw Rebecca at one of those parties. And before you ask, no, they didn't tell the police. I did when I found out, but she'd already been gone for more than ten years by then, so, needless to say, ten-year-old rumors didn't do much to further the investigation into her murder."

Pat opened his mouth as if to say something, then closed it again, ran a hand over his beard and jammed his hands into his pockets.

Rachel's hand shook as she lifted her still damp hair from where it clung to her neck threatening to strangle her. "Looking back, I know it wasn't the smartest thing I've ever done, but I was so angry, so upset, so…"

At a loss for words to describe the feelings that had overwhelmed her, she simply lifted her hands, then let them drop to her sides. "I didn't know what to do, but I couldn't do nothing, so I confronted Golino."

Pat's eyes widened.

"I went in undercover, pretended to be a runaway looking to make a few bucks. I didn't wear makeup, kept my hair stringy and pulled it over my face most of the time. Between that and my slight build, I was able to appear younger than my twenty-four years. But I was impatient, couldn't bide my time long enough to look around, maybe wait for a party and talk to some of the other women and girls, get a feel for the situation. None of them that were there then would have been there at the time Rebecca was anyway, so I figured they wouldn't know anything about her disappearance. If I had to do it again, I'd handle things differently."

He shrugged it off. "You know what they say about hindsight being twenty-twenty and all that."

"I suppose." But his understanding made the telling easier. "So, anyway, the first chance I got, I confronted Golino, asked him if he remembered my sister, shoved her picture under his nose, practically accused him of her murder. He didn't even look at it, just had his goons drag me out."

"They just let you go?"

"No. I thought for sure they'd kill me. But Ben walked in as they were escorting me, and, well, I don't know exactly where they'd have taken me, but Ben made them release me, told me to wait in the hall outside Golino's office. He wasn't in there long, but I heard yelling. Ben screamed at Golino that I knew how to keep my mouth shut, said he'd make sure of it. Then Golino shouted that he'd better be right, and the door swung open. When Ben came out, he said Golino ordered me to be set free. He walked me to the door without saying a word. When he opened the door, he grabbed my arm, stared at me with…" She paused, remembering the anger, the hatred, she'd seen in his eyes and forced a whisper out past the pain. "He looked at me like he hated me, told me to get out and never come back. He wouldn't be able to save me a second time."

"What did you do?"

She shrugged, the memories dredging up a portion of her past that was too painful, too shameful to wallow in, then told the rest quickly. "I did what he said. I walked away. I let it go. And I kept my mouth shut."

Pat stood, crossed the few steps to her and pulled her into his arms.

For just an instant, she started to back away, then sank into his embrace instead. His heart beat strong beneath her ear. She would take this—this one moment of comfort to ease the pain of remembering, of saying it all out loud for the first time ever.

"You were young, Rachel. You did what you could. You went to the police, went into Golino's undercover." He snorted out a laugh and shook his head. "Ah, man, Rachel. Anyway, in the end, there was nothing you could do."

"No, there wasn't. Not then."

He kept her in his arms but shifted her back so he could look down into her eyes. "And now?"

"I'm not letting go this time, Pat. I might not be able to get justice for Rebecca, may never know the truth—though I suspect I'm pretty close to having it right—but if there's any chance in the world I can save Jane and take down Golino, I have every intention of doing so."

"Okay."

"Okay?" She took a step back, looked hard into his eyes to gauge his reaction.

"Yeah."

"Look, Pat, I understand completely if you don't want to go ahead with this. I'll sneak out of here and head to the train station, and you can wait a little while, then leave by yourself in the SUV. They'll probably figure the woman is still inside and isn't me, and maybe they'll leave you alone."

"There is zero chance that's happening. A snake like Golino needs to be brought to justice." He kissed the top of her head, brushed her hair back from her face and grinned. "So, it looks like we're going out the side window after all. How far is the train station?"

Between the train's rocking motion and the rhythmic *clack, clack, clack*, Pat couldn't keep his eyes open. As he drifted along the precipice between wakefulness and sleep with Rachel's weight slumped against his side, he tried to force his mind to rest…to no avail. Despite having been up all night, he couldn't turn his thoughts off.

How had he gotten into this mess? Sure, he often risked his life as a rescue worker and a firefighter, had even been injured on the job, but this—going up against Long Island's most notorious crime boss—was something else entirely, something he wasn't sure he was equipped to handle.

He shifted slightly, careful not to disturb Rachel, and slitted one eye open to keep track of any newcomers boarding the train as it slowed to stop at the next station. Only two more stops, and they'd be back in Seaport, where they could borrow yet another car. He'd already called Jack and told him where he'd left his SUV, and Jack had said he'd retrieve it later in the day when, hopefully, their pursuers would have given up and left. They obviously didn't really expect Rachel to return home, or they'd have left more than the one vehicle in the parking lot to keep watch. As it was, it had been easy enough to sneak out the side window and head through the back of the apartment complex toward the train station.

Speaking of things he wasn't equipped to handle, he glanced at Rachel. He'd always been so sure he wouldn't get close to someone, would never trust someone enough to break his heart as his mother had. And yet… He'd be lying to himself if he didn't admit Rachel touched some part of him he'd believed dead or, at the very least, broken.

He shook off the thought, turned away from the fact that she seemed like a good person, the fact that he admired her. Instead, he turned to his own trust issues. While he'd been happy to see his father go, his mother had been a different story. Her abandonment had broken something in him—hurt in a way he'd never fully recovered from. If the woman he'd trusted most in life, the one he'd depended on, could hurt him so badly, how could he believe any other woman wouldn't do the same? He couldn't. It was that simple.

With that settled, and comfortable with the fact that his attraction to Rachel would no longer be a distraction, he tried once again to still his mind and rest. He let the train's motion soothe him, let his thoughts drift.

And they drifted right back to Rachel. Annoyed with himself, he lurched upright, startling Rachel from where she'd been dozing with her head against his shoulder.

Eyes wide, she looked around, braced for trouble.

"Everything's all right," Pat assured her, guilt for having disturbed her sleep annoying him even further. "I'm sorry I woke you."

"No." She sat up straighter, rubbed her eyes. "It's fine. Where are we?"

"Two more stops until Seaport."

"Did you get in touch with Jack about his SUV?"

"Yeah, it's fine. He'll pick it up later."

She frowned, narrowed her gaze on him. "You okay?"

He blew out a breath and turned his attention out the window to watch the snow-covered miles pass. The newly fallen blanket of snow was so beautiful, unmarred by footprints, tire tracks, piles of plowed dirt, snow, slush. Even the most neglected neighborhoods took on a certain charm when buried beneath the pristine snow yet to be disturbed, churned up, turned into blackened piles of sludge. It wouldn't last long. "Sorry, I didn't mean to be short with you. I'm just tired."

"Were you able to sleep at all?"

"I dozed a little." Not really a lie, though it wasn't restful. And he didn't want to add concern for him to her already cumbersome burdens. He caught himself, suddenly realizing he wanted to earn her trust, probably more than he should, and lying, by omission or otherwise, wasn't the way to do that. *Ugh.* He needed rest. Needed his life back. Needed Rachel to move on to whatever would come next for her. "How about you? Did you get any sleep?"

"A little." A moment of awkward silence passed when Pat began to pull away from her, and she probably wondered what was going on with him.

Thankfully, her phone rang.

After a quick glance at the number on the screen, she shook her head and answered. "Hello?"

Pat held his breath, tried to listen, but couldn't make out anything more than a feminine voice.

Rachel slumped against the seat back and hissed, "Where are you?"

Jane? Ben? No, a woman's voice, so not Ben.

"Okay, just stay put, I'm on my way." She stuffed the phone into her jacket pocket. "It was Shannon returning my call. She's in Watchogue waiting out the storm with friends in an empty summer home a few miles from the shack where I first found Jane."

"Okay." He nodded then leaned his head back and closed his eyes. *Please, God, help me. I've always trusted You, always tried to follow the path You've laid out for me, always tried to serve You, but right now, I'm at a loss as to what to do. Jane has disappeared. Shannon may be in danger. And Rachel might well be on her way to getting herself killed. And I feel helpless to save any of them.*

Rachel nudged his ribs gently with her elbow. "Don't get too comfortable—we're getting off soon."

He rubbed his burning eyes and sat up straighter. She was right. There was no sense in trying to get any rest. He'd just have to see this through first. "I wasn't trying to sleep, just praying."

Her eyes widened in surprise, and she tilted her head. "Do you pray often?"

"I do."

She hesitated, then asked softly, "Does God answer your prayers?"

"I like to think so." He studied her for a moment, took in her somber expression. Since her interest seemed more than just idle curiosity, he expanded. "But it's not really answers I look for when I pray, at least, not always. Sometimes it's just a comfort to realize God's with me, that I'm not alone, you know?"

She twisted on the seat, scooting away from him to turn so she could face him full on. "I prayed tonight. For the first time since Rebecca's body was found."

She paused, looked down at her hands, but he waited her out.

"I'm not sure God was listening." She sucked in a deep breath, sighed and spoke quietly. "I mean, I really do believe He led us to you, but in general, I think He may have given up on me a long time ago."

Pat smiled. He might be on shaky ground where his feelings for Rachel were concerned, but this was a subject he had firm views on. "What makes you think that?"

"I feel…" She hesitated, seemed to be searching for the right words. He wondered if that came from being a journalist, having to always choose her words carefully, and he had a sudden interest in seeing some of her work. "Empty, I guess is the best I can describe it, as if God has abandoned me. Not that I blame Him, really."

Pat took her hand, rubbed his thumb over her knuckles. "Are you sure what you're feeling is empty and not closed off? Because I feel like God is always with us, but it's a choice whether or not to let Him into your heart."

She nodded then, offered a tentative shaky smile. "I hadn't thought of it that way, but maybe you're right."

"Like any other important relationship, it's based on

love and trust." He weaved his fingers between hers, gripped her hand tighter and stared out the window to search for any sign of Golino's men as the train slowed to pull into the next station. "And like any relationship, it can be repaired if damaged."

"Thank you for that." She squeezed his hand, stood and leaned over his shoulder to see past him out the window. "Looks like I'll have to spend some time contemplating that once this is all done."

Pat stiffened at the sight of two men dressed in black business suits and dress shoes standing on the platform watching the train come in. If they were waiting for a westbound train heading into Penn Station, their attire probably wouldn't stand out as much. As it was, they were already pretty far out on Long Island, and most people heading past this point at this time of year on the heels of a major snowstorm would probably be dressed more appropriately for the weather. "In the meantime, you may want to open up and give asking for help a shot, because I have a feeling we're going to need it."

Pat lost sight of the two men as they boarded the train a few cars ahead of him and Rachel.

Rachel plopped down on the seat beside him. "Do you think they're Golino's men?"

"Probably." He looked around the car as the train started forward again, searching for any escape. Nothing. There was no way to get off while the train was moving. Only one more stop to go, but they had to stay out of sight until then.

"But how would they know we got on a train?"

He'd been contemplating the same thing even as she

said it, and he could only come up with one explanation. "They must have realized we left the Brinkmans' apartment and followed the tracks to the train station."

"What are we going to do?"

The shakiness in her voice gripped his attention, and he turned to her.

She clenched her jaw tight, but not before he caught her chin quivering.

"Hey, we're going to be okay. We'll just..." As he said the words, one of the men entered the car through the connecting door, paused and studied each of the passengers in turn. Panicked, with nowhere to run, Pat did the only thing he could think of. He yanked Rachel into his arms, cradled the back of her head and kissed her.

She stiffened in his arms, and he had a moment of fear she'd pull away and cause a scene, but then she sank into him, kissed him back, weaved her arms around his neck. And for just an instant, his eyes fluttered closed, and he lost himself in the lingering kiss, lost himself in her scent, her taste, forgot about everything but holding Rachel in his arms. He pulled her closer, intent on protecting her. *Protecting her?* It was that thought that snapped him back to reality.

He had to protect her. Shifting so he could see past her, he slitted one eye open.

The man had already walked past them as the train, nearing their stop, started to slow.

Pat gripped both of Rachel's upper arms. Noticing the tremors tearing through her, he pressed his forehead against hers. "It's okay, Rachel. He's gone."

"He?" She shook her head, narrowed her eyes at him, and started to pull away. "Gone?"

"No wait," he whispered and nearly pulled her closer for another kiss. "I don't know where his partner went."

"I…um…" She closed her eyes for a moment, then inhaled deeply, lifted her head from his and averted her gaze. "Okay, uh…"

A number of passengers stood and started to gather their belongings. If they were going to try to lose themselves amongst them, they had to get going, but he couldn't take the awkwardness between them, didn't want to leave things as they were. And didn't dare admit to himself that the kiss had been anything more than a distraction to keep them safe from Golino's men.

"I'm sorry, Rachel, I didn't mean to—"

"No." She pulled back, held up a hand between them. "It's okay. It's fine, I understand. We should go."

"Yeah." He shoved a hand through his hair, wondering how he'd ever make her feel comfortable with him again, and followed her into the aisle. He leaned forward as they closed in on the station, determined to set things right. "Rachel, I—"

"Move and you die."

Pat froze. Even without turning, he could sense the bulky man behind him, blocking any chance of escape.

"When the train stops, move with the other passengers across the platform to the black SUV waiting in the pickup lane." The man leaned closer, his hot breath against the back of Pat's neck, making his skin crawl. "Make one move, you or the woman, and I will shoot, no matter how many innocent civilians get caught in the crossfire. Understand?"

Pat nodded, his mind racing through and discarding one escape plan after another at warp speed.

"Good. Make sure the woman complies too."

He nodded again, braced his hand against a seat back as the station came into sight. He'd only have one chance, a fraction of a second, to time this right. He sucked in a deep breath, held it for an instant to calm his nerves and breathed out slowly.

The train braked, forcing all those standing to lean forward. In that instant, Pat braced against the seat, then shoved backward with all his strength. Leading with his elbow, he swung and caught his attacker in the throat.

Startled, the man staggered back.

And Pat followed through with a vicious roundhouse, throwing all of his weight behind the punch. As the man went down, Pat plowed his foot into the side of the guy's knee, dropping him instantly.

He bent and retrieved the man's weapon as it skittered across the floor, then turned and shoved Rachel forward into the bustle of panicked passengers trying to flee the scene of the fight. "Go."

EIGHT

Rachel blindly followed Pat's command—she refused to think of it as obeying an order—to shove her way through the other passengers gathered in the vestibule, cross through the gangway connection into the next car and pace herself so as not to draw unnecessary attention.

She'd been distracted by confusion over her reaction to Pat's unexpected show of affection, which, as it turned out, was only a ruse to avoid Golino's thugs. Rachel hadn't even noticed the man come up on them. But she had seen Pat take the guy out, so it didn't take a rocket scientist to figure out they'd been found.

As the train came to a full stop, she spotted a black SUV against the curb amid a line of other cars and taxis.

Golino's men? She couldn't be sure, but at least one of them had his window open, and they both peered below the visors to watch the train.

On a normal morning, the train car would be packed. This morning, not so much.

"What do you want to do?" There was no way to lose

themselves in the crowd, so they needed a plan B, and they needed it fast.

Pat pulled her hood up over her head. "Bundle yourself up as much as possible."

"You don't think that'll look suspicious?" But even as she said it, she looked around at the other passengers doing the same. While the worst of the snow had stopped, the bitterly cold wind still held a bite.

"We have to split up," Pat whispered, his gaze darting everywhere at once.

"Split up?" After running the options through her head at lightning speed, she had to agree.

"I don't know if the guy I took out communicated to anyone that he'd found us, but either way, they'll be looking for a man and a woman traveling together. You get off first, and I'll follow." He swiped a hand over his beard, glanced over his shoulder as they stopped in the vestibule.

Rachel bristled. There he went again, flipping orders, though she had to admit, in this case, he was probably right. And he wasn't really issuing orders, just stating what made the most sense. Yet the flare of annoyance the demand brought was easier to deal with than the other emotions crowding her mind, making it hard for her to think. Better, for now, to just do as he said, follow her instincts for the moment and save any real thinking for later. Besides, if she was being honest with herself, her problem with doing what she was told came from feeling helpless to do anything but what she was told when Rebecca disappeared. Another thought for later.

"There's a railroad yard just east of the station. Walk

straight across the street with the crowd that will un-doubtedly head to the café on the corner for coffee, then you should be able to slip unnoticed around the back and into the yard. It's fenced, so you'll have to walk along the tracks to enter. Make sure you watch out for the train."

She nodded, mapping his directions in her mind since she was not at all familiar with the area.

"Once you get into the yard, there's plenty of equip-ment for cover: trains waiting to go out, large storage containers, trailers. Just keep walking along the tracks, and I'll catch up with you."

Keeping her head down, hands in her pockets, and hood pulled low over her face, she slid between a teen-ager carrying a duffle bag and a woman with a crying infant, then inched forward toward the door as the train finally came to a complete stop. A quick peek out the window showed the two men still sitting in place, scru-tinizing every passenger as they disembarked.

She held her breath, tried to slow her racing heart. She could do this. Plenty of people got off the train and walked. Granted, most of them didn't do so in close to a foot of snow, but if she tried to appear casual, maybe in just a bit of a hurry because of the weather, she might be able to pull it off. The key would be not to draw attention to herself, to pace herself with the others who'd cross the street to the café, to blend in. While the woman with the wailing infant was a good distrac-tion, she needed something more.

She yanked her phone out of her pocket and pressed it against her ear as if talking to someone. Using her arm to cover most of her face, she ducked against the wind and stepped off the train onto the platform. She muttered to herself as she hurried down the stairs and onto the sort of cleared sidewalk, careful not to slide in the sandy, salty slush. It probably would have been safer if they'd just left the snow alone. If she went down in this mess, she would surely draw the men's attention.

While she didn't dare risk turning to look at the two men, she did twist to the side and glance over her other shoulder in time to see Pat disappear around the back of the train.

She wasn't sure she agreed with Pat's assessment of her relationship with God, but she was willing to try to open up more, to let God's presence guide her, comfort her. And this was as good a time as any to start. "God, please keep Pat safe. And thank you for sending him to help."

Even if that help did come with a kiss that had left her momentarily shaken.

Her foot slid, and she scrambled to stay upright and keep her phone from dropping into a puddle of slush. She started to turn and look behind her to see if anyone had noticed, then caught herself and looked straight ahead as she regained her footing and stepped off the curb into the parking lot. If she kept her mind off Pat and on what she was doing, she might even survive the day.

The whistle of the locomotive startled her, and she jumped as it began to inch forward. She'd hoped to make it to the yard before everyone had disembarked and she was more likely to be noticed. Now, she'd have to wait until after the train passed to walk along the tracks. She increased her pace as she crossed the street and slid between two stopped cars waiting for the gates to open once the train went by. Hopefully, she'd put enough space between her and Golino's men to be out of view.

She slowed in front of the café, where a couple of people lingered, huddled beneath the overhang, probably waiting for rides. The instant the last train car passed through the fence surrounding the yard, Rachel hurried toward the tracks, then plowed through a deep snowdrift and behind the cover of a large tractor-trailer-style storage container.

Confident she could no longer be seen from the parking lot, she looked around for Pat and spotted him walking parallel to her on the far side of the tracks. A wave of relief, followed by something else she couldn't quite name, poured over her as she waited for him to catch up.

When he reached her, winded, he bent at the waist, propped his hands on his knees and sucked in deep, greedy breaths.

Concern for his well-being pushed everything else to the background, and she laid a hand on his back, scanned the area for signs of anyone in pursuit. "Are you okay? Are you hurt?"

He nodded as he straightened. "Yeah. Come on. We have to go."

One of his knuckles had split, and he was favoring his right leg, but other than that, he seemed okay. Sharing his sense of urgency, she started in the direction he indicated. The questions currently battering her would have to wait until they'd found somewhere safe to talk.

"Can you climb the fence?" he hissed between ragged breaths.

Maybe he was hurt worse than she realized. But, still, they had to get out of there. The firehouse couldn't be too far. Surely there would be someone who could look him over there. A quick glance at the ice-coated six-foot chain-link fence had her stomach turning over. "Can't we just follow the tracks to the next opening?"

"We can if you can't climb it, but the snow is really churned up here from employees coming and going, and we have a better chance of getting out without anyone being able to follow our tracks."

That made sense. Initially, she'd hoped the storm would make it easier for them to get away, but so far, the fact they left a trail everywhere they went hadn't worked to their advantage. Maybe they could change that. "Yeah, sure, I can climb it."

She scrambled up a pile of ice-packed snow someone had plowed against the fence, then got a good hold on the links. She hadn't climbed a fence since she was a kid and Ben had challenged her to see who could get over faster. He'd won, of course, and she'd ended up with a bloody scrape up her side and a bruised ego. The memory almost brought a smile before the reality of what Ben had become intruded on the moment.

She shoved the thought away and concentrated on scaling the fence without losing her footing. Once she got over the top, she dropped to the ground beside Pat, who had somehow beat her over despite having started after her.

He pulled out his phone as he started walking.

Rachel looked around. "I'm not familiar with the area at all, but didn't we pass Seaport town? Isn't the firehouse the other way?"

"Yeah, but we can't go back there. I'm going to have one of the guys bring Shadow and meet us with a car."

She stuck her hands into her jacket pockets and trudged beside him, sulking over the thought he'd only kissed her as a distraction, though she'd never admit that out loud, could barely even admit it to herself.

The call didn't last long, leaving them huffing along in silence.

Once Pat had his breath back, he stopped. "Look, Rachel, I just want to apologize for what happened back there."

She had no choice but to stop and face him. She lifted her chin. No way would she let him see how the kiss had affected her. Better to just keep her feelings to herself, get through this nightmare and move on with the business of living her life. A new story; that's what she needed. Something to distract her. Maybe a story about firefighters, or even better, the use of rescue dogs in— She caught herself, and heat flared in her cheeks. "It's fine, Pat. I said I understand."

He started to reach for her, then put his hands into his pockets instead. "I'm not sure you do."

Wrapping her arms around herself for comfort as well as warmth, Rachel gave him space to think. He clearly had something on his mind, and since they were waiting for someone to show up with a car anyway, the deserted neighborhood seemed like a quiet enough place to catch their breath.

"When I kissed you…" He looked away, clearly miserable.

At least she wasn't alone there. A smile tugged at Rachel's lips, and she bit it back.

"It's not that… Look…" He finally reached for her, rubbed his hands up and down her arms then let his hands fall to his sides when she kept her arms firmly locked around herself. "I'd be lying if I didn't admit I find you attractive, admire you, respect you, even have feelings I don't really understand and can't examine at this point in my life. If we'd met under other circumstances or at a different point in time, I might feel differently, but right now, I'm not ready for or interested in a relationship. Friendship, yes, for sure, but nothing more than that. At the moment, I'm just trying to find my own purpose in life. That's one of the things that drove me to seek the solitude of my uncle's cabin while I recuperated."

She glued her eyes to his despite the spark of pain and regret his words ignited.

"I'm sorry if I ever led you to believe anything other than that."

She forced a smile. "Good. Okay, that's good."

He lifted a brow. "It is?"

"Yes, because I feel the same way." Though the twisting in her gut belied the words she uttered to him and to herself.

"You do?"

"I'm damaged, Pat." At least that was true enough. "And I'm not sure I'll ever be able to trust someone enough to have a lasting relationship with them. I've spent years concentrating on my work, trying to... I don't know...do right by others, I guess, since I wasn't able to save Rebecca."

He started to protest, but she held up a hand to stop him.

"I know what happened to her wasn't my fault." Though that did nothing to alleviate the guilt that she hadn't been able to prove who'd killed her and find justice for her. "But I can't help feeling I failed her in some way, and helping others helps me feel like I'm atoning for that, at least to a certain degree. So, that's where my focus is at this point in my life. Not on settling down with someone, making a home, building a family."

A pang of regret shot through her.

"I don't think those things are meant for me." She fought back the tears that desperately wanted to fall, the inner voice that begged her to rethink her decision and her priorities. This was how things needed to be. Especially since Pat felt the same way. She took a deep breath, blew it out on a cloud of vapor and smiled, confident she'd made the right choice now that she was over the initial shock at him kissing her. Hopefully her cheeks were already red from the cold, because if the burning sensation was any indication, they'd be bright red at the thought of the tenderness with which he'd held her.

"Okay then." He smiled, but it didn't quite reach his eyes, and she thought, hoped, he might have a little regret himself. "So, where do we go from here?"

"We go find Shannon, and try to rescue Jane, and put an end to this nightmare so we can move on with our lives." She hooked her arm companionably through his and started walking, then offered a more genuine smile. "And hopefully we find a way to stay friends."

"Sounds like a plan. But you have to admit…" He grinned, his eyes sparkling with mischief, sending her traitorous heart all aflutter, as he nudged her with his shoulder. "It was a great kiss."

Gabe had already taken Jack to retrieve his SUV from Rachel's apartment, then followed him out to Watchogue so Jack could lend the vehicle to Pat and Rachel again. As Pat drove the borrowed SUV, he tried not to let his disappointment show. While he'd tried to be completely honest about his feelings, he suspected some small part of him had hoped Rachel would try to push for something more. Foolish, sure, but he couldn't deny it. If he wasn't careful, this beautiful, spunky woman might just find a way through the shield he'd erected years ago—one that no one had been able to breach since his mother had destroyed him when she'd left.

And that is so not happening. He'd help Rachel, Jane and even Shannon, if they could convince her, out of this mess and then go back to his life. Or maybe move on to something else. Either way, whatever decision he made, it wouldn't involve any woman long term.

When his mother had left, he'd been so sure she'd return that he'd lie awake half the night listening for the front door to open, watching for her to crack his bedroom door and peer into his room, apologize for the mistake she made leaving him. He'd throw his arms around her, lose himself in the scent of the perfume she always wore and forgive her. Then they'd move on as if nothing had happened. To this day the scent of jasmine still brought a jolt of pain, had him pausing, holding his breath and looking around in search of the woman who'd broken his heart.

"Slow down." Rachel's voice startled him from his misery. "You have to make a right up here."

"Huh? Oh, yeah, thanks."

She frowned. "Are you sure you're okay?"

He shook off the lingering sadness. "I am, yes. Sorry, just tired and a bit sore. It's been a while since I've done anything quite so physically demanding."

"You didn't get hurt when you fought with that guy?"

"Nope. I'm fine. Caught him off guard, and he never even landed a punch. Nothing more than a twinge in my leg where I was injured and a few scraped knuckles." Although now, not only did they have to worry about Golino's men finding them, but they had to worry about the police as well, since Gabe had informed him a concerned citizen with a cell phone camera had caught the entire incident on video.

"Are you sure we did the right thing involving Gabe in this?" Rachel stared out the windshield, absently chewing on her lower lip.

"We had no choice, Rachel. You have to try to talk Shannon into going with him."

She nodded but still didn't look fully convinced.

"We can't protect her, especially if we're still going to look for Jane. We already have targets painted on our backs. Do you really want to put her in Golino's sights too?" He'd second-guessed the plan enough times to understand her hesitation, to be thoroughly familiar with all of the arguments both for and against. Since Jack and Gabe were sitting in a small parking lot in town waiting to hear from Pat if Shannon would agree to go with them, they had to at least try to convince her. It might be the only way to keep her safe.

"She might already be on his radar if anyone suspects she was the one to leak the information that led me to finding Jane."

"Exactly. Which is why we have to convince her to go with Jack and Gabe." He reached for her hand just as she lifted it to rub her eyes, then let his own fall. It was probably for the best. While he'd have liked to offer reassurance, he wouldn't want to give her the wrong impression.

"Are you going to leave Shadow with them when we're done here?"

He massaged his temples where a dull ache had begun to throb toward a full-blown migraine. "It depends on where we decide to go next, but I'd prefer to take him with us. I don't like being away from him for so long."

"There." She pointed toward a large stone house surrounded by a wrought iron fence. "That's the house. Shannon said you have to follow the fence around the back, then walk in from the beach."

Pat followed her directions, getting the SUV as close to the fence as possible on the unplowed road. He pocketed the key, then strode to the end of the fence and onto the low dunes. While the bay remained choppy, at least the waves had lessened, leaving the beach clear enough to walk on.

Deep yellows and oranges streaked the sky like flames as the sun inched toward the bay. The thought of heading down to Florida to check in on his uncle when this was done, maybe sitting on a warm beach and watching the sun dip below the horizon, flashed through his mind. The fact that Rachel sat beside him in the image his mind conjured annoyed him, and he shook the thought off. He had no business envisioning Rachel at his side when he could offer her nothing. It wasn't like he was going to marry her…or anyone else.

With his hands in his pockets, he hunched against the cold wind-whipped spray coming off the water. His mother and father must have loved each other once upon a time, right? They'd married, after all, had a child, must have tried to build a life together. So, what had gone wrong? How could they have gone from a young couple in love to two people who could barely stand to be in the same room with each other over the course of only a few years? And even once they'd divorced… Sure, his father had moved on, made a life with a new wife, a new family, but what of his mother? She'd remained bitter, angry, broken. Her time with his father, the pain he'd caused her, had so thoroughly damaged her that it had also destroyed any hope of a close relationship with her own child.

Even if he and Rachel did try to make a go of it, what's to say the same thing wouldn't happen to the two of them? Rachel was headstrong and Pat was set in his ways. What if he did decide to risk his heart and take a chance with Rachel, and they couldn't make it work? No, Pat would never put himself in the posi-

tion of loving someone so completely that losing them
would destroy him.

He glanced across the bay to where the sun continued its descent beyond the barrier island. Another half
hour and it would be dark. Pat hoped to be out of there
before that happened.

"She said to wait here." Rachel slogged to the corner of the yard and stopped in knee-deep snow beside
a stone pillar, then followed his gaze out over the bay.

The urge to grip her hand, or even tuck her beneath
his arm, and pause to enjoy the more-colorful-than-
usual sunset nearly overwhelmed him. He ignored it.
"Did you text her we're here?"

"I did." She caught her bottom lip between her teeth
and glanced at him from beneath her lashes.

"What's the matter?"

"I was just lost in my own thoughts. Do you think—"

"Rachel." The low hiss interrupted them as a young
girl who probably hadn't hit seventeen stepped out from
the shadows.

"Shannon." Rachel reached for her, gripped her arms
and stood facing her as she gave her a quick once-over.
"Are you all right?"

Shannon nodded, tumbling a mane of black hair into
her face. She wrapped her arms around her thin frame,
her teeth chattering. Her gaze skipped to Pat, who Rachel had already warned her was coming, then back
to Rachel. Hope filled her tumultuous dark eyes. "Did
you find Jane?"

Rachel shook her head, rubbed her hands up and

down Shannon's arms then released her. "Not yet, but we will. Shannon, you have to listen to me."

The girl pulled her oversized sweatshirt sleeves down over her hands and hunched closer to a brick column.

"We have somewhere safe for you to hide, but you need to come with us now."

Shannon looked back toward the house.

Pat held his breath, praying she wouldn't make a scene, especially since they had no clue how many people might be inside the house and how many of them might be armed. And how many of them might have a connection to Golino, considering he often used runaways for a variety of odd jobs. That's all they needed— one ambitious thug looking for a quick run up the gangster ladder.

While Rachel still had the handgun in her jacket pocket, Pat had left the shotgun in the car. Although most of the area was deserted this time of year, especially during a storm, there was no telling when some concerned citizen might look out his window and spot him trudging through the neighborhood lugging a shotgun and call the police.

"Alec told me to wait here." Her gaze flickered to Pat, toward the beach and back to Rachel. "He didn't come back yet."

"Shannon..." Rachel hesitated and glanced at Pat.

If she knew Alec wasn't going to return, she might agree to going with them. On the other hand, if she knew he'd been killed, she might just take off and disappear. Figuring it was best to just be honest, he nodded.

Rachel sucked in a breath, exhaled a cloud of vapor. "I'm sorry, Shannon. Alec was killed last night."

"You killed him?" she whispered with a glance over her shoulder.

"No! Uh…" She winced and lowered her voice. "I mean, no, it wasn't me. One of Golino's guys took him out after I escaped with Jane."

Her eyes narrowed in suspicion. "I thought you said you didn't have Jane."

This was not going well. Pat had agreed to let Rachel do the talking, but every instinct he'd honed over the past years begged him to get going. He eyed Rachel, let his gaze bore into hers in an effort to hurry her along. If the clock ticking away in his head was any indication, they were running out of time fast.

"We don't. I mean, we did, but we lost her. Please, Shannon, just come with us, and I'll explain everything."

She narrowed her gaze even further, eyed Pat from the corner of her eyes. "That's what you said when you called, that you'd explain everything when you got here. Well. Here you are. Start explaining."

Seemingly the picture of patience, though Pat suspected her outward calm was a vast contradiction to the sense of urgency raging inside her, Rachel nodded. "I did, yes. Okay. Short version, I found Jane where you said. She'd been drugged. Golino's men came after us, killed Alec and another guy and chased us. We ran into Pat." She gestured toward him. "And he helped us escape. Then Jane took off, and Golino's men got her."

Since Rachel had brought him into the conversation,

sort of, he figured it was okay to offer his two cents. "We have to get out of here, Shannon. Please, we can take you somewhere safe where Rachel and I will explain everything. You returned Rachel's call because you trusted her, and you're concerned for your friend. Well, your friend is still in danger, and Rachel and I are trying to help, but we can't if you won't come with us and tell us everything you know. Let us help Jane. Let us protect you. Please."

Shannon seemed to consider him for a moment, then turned to Rachel and nodded.

Relief weakened Pat's knees. "Come on."

When Shannon fell into step beside Rachel, with one last glance over her shoulder at the house, Pat shifted to walk on her other side. If they kept the young girl between them, there was less chance she'd get away if she got spooked and ran.

It didn't take them long to reach the vehicle. Keeping his head on a swivel, Pat unlocked the door, ushered Shannon and Rachel inside, then rounded the SUV and slid into the driver's seat. He didn't dare breathe a sigh of relief until they'd driven up and down a few random blocks and made it onto Main Street. At least the storm ending had a few most likely year-round residents out and about, making their presence less obvious if they were spotted. Instead of heading straight toward Gabe and Jack, Pat weaved through the quiet town.

Rachel turned in her seat to look back at Shannon. "Shannon, when Jane was with us, she said something happened with Carmine Golino. We think whatever it was is the reason she's in danger right now. Do you know what happened between them?"

Pat watched closely in the rearview mirror for her reaction. When she started to shiver uncontrollably, he shifted the vent to face her more fully and turned up the heat.

She lifted one brow. "Jane told you that, about Golino?"

Twisting farther in her seat, Rachel looked more fully into Shannon's eyes. "She did, yes."

"Why would she confide in you?"

"Because we promised her we'd find you and protect you if she told us what was going on. Now, don't you think it's only fair you do the same for her?"

The demand seemed a bit heavy-handed to Pat, but who knew? Maybe that's what was needed at this point, so he remained quiet.

Shannon nodded once, the motion barely perceptible.

"Tell me. Please, Shannon," Rachel pleaded.

When Shannon simply shifted to look out the window, Rachel turned back around and slumped in the seat.

The soft crunch of ice beneath the tires whispered around them. Pat had no clue where to go. The best thing would probably be to drop Shannon with Gabe and Jack, who were waiting nearby, and let them protect her. If she'd even go with them. Until then, though, if Shannon refused to talk, he and Rachel were wasting time that might be better spent hitting the streets in search of any information about where Jane might have been taken.

Not that he had any idea where to look. Unless...

"Look, Rachel, why don't we pick up Shadow? Chances are Golino's men are long gone from the vacation cabin Jane took off from." They'd have no reason to hang around once Pat and Rachel got away, no reason to think they'd return once they'd escaped. "If we go back to the spot Jane was last seen, he can most likely track her."

She nodded absently, her attention seeming to be a million miles away. "You really think he can find her?"

He shrugged. He had no doubt Shadow could track her from where she'd been abducted, but... "He can track her to the point where they switched her to a vehicle, but who knows? There may be a clue to their whereabouts. If nothing else, at least we'd have a direction to start looking in."

She closed her eyes, rubbed at them with a thumb and forefinger. He could almost feel her frustration.

"You won't find her," Shannon said so quietly he almost missed it.

He glanced in the rearview mirror, caught Shannon's gaze and looked into eyes way older than her years. "Why not?"

"They would have taken her back to the boat. She's probably long gone by now."

"You think they'd have returned to the same spot Rachel first found her?"

She shrugged one slim shoulder. "No reason not to."

"They can't know whether or not we called the police."

She scoffed. "Yeah, like that would matter."

Rachel stiffened beside him. "What do you mean?"

She huffed out a breath and flung her arms to the sides, for the first time looking like the recalcitrant teenager she should have had a chance to be, then let them drop at her sides. "That's what caused the problems for Jane in the first place."

"Cops?"

"*A* cop. The detective who killed that witness."

Pat's heart stuttered.

Rachel went dead pale. "Detective?"

"Yeah, Harrison. Ben or Brad or something like that. Jane was at Golino's house for a party, keeping her head down like I taught her, serving drinks, cleaning up... whatever else Golino needed doing, and the detective came in with the witness."

"Are you sure the detective killed him?"

"Her. The witness was a woman—a woman who worked directly for Golino for years. Gemma Bertolino. She'd gotten out, was set to testify, when the cop brought her to Golino, and he ordered the hit and walked out as if that woman's life meant absolutely nothing."

Rachel squeezed her eyes closed. This couldn't be easy on her. "Did Jane actually see him kill her? The cop?"

"She didn't actually see him fire, but..." Shannon shrugged and picked at the loose threads fraying her sweatshirt sleeves. "He was the only one in the room when he put the gun to her head, and Jane said she closed her eyes and ducked behind the couch, afraid she'd be next. She heard the gunshot, saw the body wrapped in plastic when he hefted it over his shoulder and walked out. I don't know about you, but it seems pretty clear to me he did her in."

Tears tracked down Rachel's cheeks as she stared straight ahead out the windshield.

To give her a moment to collect herself, Pat asked quietly, "So, Ben Harrison is what? Golino's hit man?"

"More like his exterminator."

"But why wait until now? The trial was a few years ago, wasn't it? If the witness was killed back then, why come after Jane now?"

"Word is, Golino's got a weasel in his house, and the cops are coming after him again, this time with even more ammo. So the man's cleaning house, getting rid of any potential rats before the infestation can destroy him."

Pat blew out a breath. Jane's chances of survival just went barreling downhill. "I have a couple of friends, Shannon. They will keep you safe."

She snorted. "Nowhere's safe."

Seemingly having collected herself, Rachel wiped the tears from her cheeks and turned to face the frightened young girl—because that's what Shannon was. Despite her composure, the terror reflected in her eyes was unmistakable. "Shannon, please. Alec is gone, which means even if he could have protected you from Golino, he can't now. If anyone puts two and two together, which really shouldn't be too difficult, they will figure it was you who ratted them out. Especially since Ben Harrison saw me at the scene and recognized me. They will figure it out."

Shannon laid her head back, seemed to stare a million miles past the roof of the car.

"Let us help you. Please," Rachel begged.

Pat turned toward town. He was done. Jane might be lost to them, either for the moment or for good, but he would not see Shannon face the same fate. Gabe could arrest her and lead her away in handcuffs for all he cared, but he was not sending her back out onto the street to be exterminated with the rest of Golino's perceived threats.

NINE

Relieved that they'd been able to talk Shannon into accepting help, Rachel climbed out of the SUV and waited for Pat and Shannon to do the same. As they started toward Gabe's SUV, where Gabe and Jack sat waiting, Rachel's phone rang. One look at the caller ID had her heart stuttering to a standstill. Ben Harrison. "Shannon, I have to take this, but I promise I'll do everything I can to find Jane."

Shannon only nodded and looked miserable, hands stuffed in her sweatshirt pockets, eyes cast downward as Pat led her to Gabe.

Unfortunately, Rachel didn't have time to reassure her. She didn't dare miss Ben's call. Even as she swiped the screen to answer, she turned away from Pat and walked back toward the borrowed SUV. "Hello?"

"Rachel." The sound of his voice brought back a wave of memories, both good and bad. "We need to talk."

She didn't dare let her guard down, couldn't afford to forget what he'd become for even an instant. "I'm listening."

"In person."

She forced a laugh. "That is so not happening, Ben."

"Please, Rachel, you don't understand."

"Then explain." And she really hoped he could. But he didn't come by the reputation as Golino's exterminator without getting blood on his hands, and she'd seen him kill two of his men with her own eyes.

"Hold on."

She strained to hear his muffled voice, but he must have covered the phone because she couldn't make out any of the conversation. A quick check showed Pat still talking to Gabe and Jack. Since Shannon had already climbed into the back seat, she assumed there was no problem.

When Pat glanced over at her and their eyes met, his were filled with questions. Questions he most likely wasn't going to get answers to since she had no intention of putting anyone else in danger if she caved and did what she suspected she was going to.

Ben had had the opportunity to kill Rachel, more than once, and he hadn't. Maybe he wouldn't or couldn't. But that same loyalty might not extend to anyone else. If she did agree to meet him, it would have to be alone. And no way was Pat going to agree to that. She shook off the guilt that she was even considering lying to him and going alone, told herself it was for his own protection, so it was probably okay. Her conscience begged to differ.

"I'm out of time, Rachel. I need you to shake your guard dog and meet me."

Guard dog? The comment rankled her.

"I'll be at the shack where you first found the girl in an hour. One hour. I won't wait more than five minutes, but if you want to save the girl, that five minutes will be your only window of opportunity. It's a narrow one, Rachel. After that, she'll be gone. Don't blow it." The line went dead.

"Ben?" Nothing. Whatever background noise she'd heard during his call had disappeared. Background noise? Something rhythmic. Tires against pavement? Was he driving? Maybe, but that didn't seem quite right.

"Is everything all right?" Pat's hand on her shoulder had her jumping about three feet in the air even as she whirled on him and let out an embarrassingly squeaky screech.

She pressed a hand against her chest to keep her heart from jumping out. "What are you trying to do to me? Scare me to death?"

He grinned, the adorable dimple denting beneath his beard. "Sorry."

She lifted a brow at him. "Funny, you don't seem the least bit sorry."

"Not that it wasn't entertaining, but I am sorry I frightened you." He gestured toward her phone. "Was that about Jane?"

The moment of truth. She stuffed the phone into her pocket. Evade or tell him the truth? Would she really only be lying to protect him? Despite what she tried to tell herself, she had a feeling there was more to her reticence. Trust? Isn't that what it all boiled down to in the end? Did she trust Pat? Could she open up and trust anyone else after Ben had betrayed her so completely? Was the possibility of saving Jane, easing her conscious even just a little over having lost Rebecca, worth risking everything and trusting him?

She already knew she couldn't trust Ben. But what if there was even the slightest possibility he was trying to help her save Jane? She wanted to scream, wanted to pull at her hair, wanted... Wanted what? Guidance.

Rachel's own words played through her head. *I'm telling you, Mom, Rebecca wouldn't have run away. You have to believe me, Dad. Something bad must have happened to her if she didn't come home...* Followed by the promise she'd made to Rebecca. *I'll find you, Rebecca. I promise. I'll keep on everyone until they bring you home.* And she hadn't been able to keep that promise. Not even after it was too late. She'd trusted then, and Rebecca had still died.

Shannon's plea followed, *No police. Promise me, or I won't tell you where to find her.* Jane's words came right on the heels of that memory. *No police. Promise?*

And she'd done as they'd asked.

And how had things turned out so far? Rebecca had been killed, Jane was missing and, if there was any truth in Ben's words, was about to disappear for good. And Shannon...

Wait. Shannon was safe. Safe with Pat's friends, because Shannon had trusted Rachel, had trusted Pat.

She inhaled deeply, blew the breath out on a slow count of ten. She hadn't realized her eyes had closed, but she opened them now, stared straight into Pat's gaze.

Could she trust him?

"So, have you decided?"

"Decided what?"

"Decided if you're going to trust me enough to tell me about the phone call you just received." His smirk unknotted the ball of tension coiled in her gut.

A smile tugged at her lips, and she lowered her gaze to hide it. No need to let him know he had her pegged so completely. "What makes you think that?"

He cleared his throat and waited for her to look up at him. When she did, he sighed. "Seriously, Rachel?"

She kept her gaze level on his until he relented.

"Okay, fine. You have tells. When you're trying to decide whether or not to share something with me." He massaged a spot on her forehead just over the bridge of her nose with his thumb. "Your forehead wrinkles up right here when you scowl." Then he lowered his hand to brush a finger over her lips. "And you chew on your lower lip."

Her breath caught.

He leaned toward her.

She started to lift onto her tiptoes, tilted her head.

"So, what's going on?" Jack blew into his hands, rubbed them together and glanced back and forth between the two of them.

Pat pulled back with a wry grin and gestured toward Rachel. "Rachel was just about to tell me that. Weren't you, Rachel?"

She didn't bother to release the sigh. He'd left her with very little choice but to come clean. Of course, she'd already pretty much decided to trust him anyway, maybe not with her heart but with her life. And Jane's. "Yeah, I guess I was, but let's at least get out of the cold. My feet are so numb I wouldn't be able to run three feet if my life depended on it."

And it might well.

Pat held the back door of Gabe's SUV open so she could slide in beside Shannon, then went around and got in on her other side. Jack climbed into the front passenger seat beside Gabe. With the heater running, all five of them packed into the smallish SUV. With Shadow in the back, leaning over Shannon's shoulder and panting, Rachel warmed up quickly. As she relayed her conversation with Ben, she unwound Jaelyn's scarf and tucked it beside her on the seat.

"Whatever you do—" Shannon was the first to speak when Rachel had finished "—don't trust him. I want Jane back, but if the exterminator has her, she's as good as dead anyway. No sense everyone else getting dead too."

But something tugged at Rachel, something just out of reach.

"So, what do you want to do?" Pat frowned at her, but she appreciated the fact that he'd asked for her opinion first.

Too bad she had no clue how to proceed. "I'm leaning toward meeting up with him."

"Of course you are." With a weary sigh, he scrubbed his hands over his face. "And are you planning to go alone as he asked?"

Rachel frowned, her mind preoccupied with whatever was bothering her. Well, this whole mess was bothering her, but something about Ben's phone call. Something he'd said? She ran through the conversation in her mind again. Nothing. It had been short and sweet: meet him at the shack if she wanted to save Jane. A quick glance at the dashboard clock told her they had to get moving. Not that they were far from the shack, since they'd gone back out to Watchogue to meet up with Shannon, but if they were going to come up with any kind of plan, it needed to be now. "What do you think, Pat?"

"I don't like it," he answered instantly, no hesitation whatsoever.

She didn't like it either, any of it, but the alternative was to give up and just let Jane die, and that was not an option. At least, not for Rachel. "But?" she prodded.

He shook his head, ran a hand through his hair and turned his gaze out the window at the darkening sky. Flurries had once again begun to fall. "I don't know what else we can do. What about you, Gabe? What do you think?"

He turned to face them and hooked an arm over the seat back. "I understand your concern about involving the police, considering the situation with Detective Harrison, and I respect your wishes. I even agree we have no clue how many other cops might be involved with Golino. But why don't I talk to my captain, get together a small group of cops I know I can trust, maybe see if there's any truth to the rumor cops are going after him? And if you're going to insist on meeting up with him anyway, we can at least send you in wearing a wire?"

Shannon was already shaking her head. "Dude's a cop. It's the first thing he'll look for before he says anything."

"Shannon's right," Rachel agreed. "Ben might be a lot of things, but stupid isn't one of them, and he'll never open his mouth and say anything incriminating without first checking for a wire."

"Probably." Gabe tapped his fingers in a steady rhythm against the back of Jack's seat.

Something about the rhythm made her think of her conversation with Ben when she tried to come up with any alternative to giving in to Ben's demands. "Okay, even if I would agree to the wire plan, we're out of time. Ben was very specific: one hour, and he'd only wait five minutes, not a second more. So we have no choice. I go in alone without wearing a wire."

A chorus of no's vetoed that.

"It's my choice." She shifted her gaze from one of them to the next. "And I'm going to meet him."

Jack and Gabe turned their focus to Pat.

Rachel did as well. "I didn't have to say anything. I could have just taken off in Jack's SUV and gone alone. Heck, I could have walked back there in an hour, but you asked me to trust you, and I did. This is me trusting you, Pat. But you have to meet me halfway. I'll agree to try to make it as safe as possible, but if I only have a five-minute window to save Jane, I'm taking it. Period. We'd better get planning because the clock's ticking."

Shadow leaned his head over the back seat and nudged Rachel's shoulder.

She nuzzled against him, reached up to cup his big head in her hand and pet him behind the ear.

"Okay." Pat pursed his lips, then slowly nodded.

"Fair enough. Rachel's right. She could have ditched us and gone alone, but she didn't."

Rachel's relief didn't last long. "So, where does that leave us?"

Jack, who'd remained quiet until then, cracked his window, allowing the flurries to swirl through the vehicle. He shrugged out of his heavy coat and turned to more easily face both Pat and Rachel in the back seat. "Gabe, why don't you take Shannon somewhere safe, somewhere you can protect her?"

Gabe looked to Shannon for approval. "Would that be okay with you?"

She glanced back and forth between Pat and Rachel, then chewed on her lower lip and nodded once.

"Okay..." Pat took the key to Jack's SUV out of his pocket and handed it to him. "But we're almost out of gas."

"Here, give it to me." Gabe held out his hand. "We'll take Jack's car and fill the tank. You guys just get going."

With that settled, Jack gave Gabe the key. "Why don't you guys go now, get out of here before anyone drives by and notices us all parked here."

He nodded and took the key. "Come on, Shannon. Let's leave these guys to save your friend."

Rachel squeezed Shannon's hand before Pat got out and held the door open for her. Confident Gabe would keep Shannon safe, Rachel watched them hurry across the lot while Pat rounded the front of the vehicle to take the driver's seat.

Alone in the back seat, Rachel shifted to rest her head against Shadow's neck, taking comfort from his

warmth. What had Pat said? We each have to find our
own path to God, or words to that effect. Well, maybe
this was hers, because in addition to trusting Pat, she
was going to trust God as well—trust He'd allowed
her to find Jane for a reason, trust He'd guide her now
to save the young girl. Maybe even trust that Pat still
had a role to play. Rachel closed her eyes and whispered softly, "God, please, don't let me fail her. Don't
let *us* fail her."

Once he slid behind the wheel, Pat turned to Jack.
"You don't have to come with us, you know. I can drop
you off at the train station."

Rachel found herself wishing they were back on the
train, the motion soothing her to—

She lurched upright.

"Nah, I think I'll stick with you guys." With a grin,
he punched Pat in the arm. "Someone's gotta keep you
out of trouble."

Then their voices faded. Rachel's mind raced. The
train. The rhythmic sound she'd heard in the background when Ben was talking to her. He'd called from
the train. Looking for them? For her? Maybe. But if he
was on the train, where was Jane? He obviously wasn't
lugging a kidnap victim around on public transporta-
tion. She'd assumed Ben had Jane with him, but she
must be at the shack with only a small window of time
before the boat showed up for her. "Guys, I don't think
Ben has Jane."

Pat's gaze shot to the rearview mirror to meet hers.
"What do you mean? Why not?"

"Because he called me from the train. What do you think the chances are he's got Jane with him?"

But Pat was already shaking his head. "No way he's got her on the train. Even with fewer than usual people traveling because of the weather, there are still enough passengers to notice a girl being held against her will."

"Unless he's got her drugged," Rachel suggested.

"Still. An unconscious teenage girl on a train, alone or with a grown man, is going to draw attention, going to ping some concerned citizen's radar. Are you sure he was on the train?"

"Positive. I heard it in the background."

Pat shifted into Reverse, turned to look out the back window and made eye contact with Rachel. "You're sure you still want to go through with this?"

What choice did she have? Besides, if Ben didn't have Jane, maybe he knew who did. Maybe he really was trying to save her. A small flicker of hope tried to surface but died just as quickly.

What had Shannon called him? The exterminator? Was he aptly named? Because he could also be setting a trap for her. Perhaps Jane was long gone, and Ben just wanted to tie up another loose end. Rachel. But then why tell her to ditch the guard dog? Wouldn't he want to kill Pat as well? He'd have to assume Pat knew just as much as Rachel did.

While Pat and Jack discussed their options and tried to work out some kind of plan, Rachel tuned them out. Whatever they decided didn't really matter to her. She had no doubt they were trying to find a way to protect her and find Jane. Maybe they could and maybe they couldn't, but she knew in her heart she had to meet with Ben. Whatever was about to happen, meeting with him was her role. But was it all about saving Jane? Mostly it was, though she could admit, at least to herself, some part of her deep down was hoping Ben would decide to do the right thing. Who knew? Maybe Pat was right. Maybe it was never too late to redeem yourself.

Tears tracked down her cheeks as Pat drove. She swiped them away. "You can drop me at my car, and I'll go on foot from there."

Pat's jaw clenched tight, and he stared straight ahead, saying nothing.

Jack studied him for a moment, then turned toward Rachel. "Shadow is the best there is. You have nothing to worry about. We're going to find Jane, and if Ben takes you anywhere, we'll be able to find you too."

"And if he shoots her the minute she walks into the clearing?" Pat asked, his tone colder than the night they'd just spent trudging through the snow in below freezing temperatures.

"You said she's got a weapon," Jack reminded him.

"Yeah, about that." Rachel slid forward, rested an elbow on each seat back and peered at Pat between the seats. She'd kept this part to herself before now, worried it would be a deal breaker. "I'm not taking the gun, I'm leaving it with you."

If the look Pat pinned her with in the mirror was any indication, it seemed she was right. He pulled up next to her car and shifted into Park, then turned to glare at her. "Not happening."

"Hear me out."

"No."

"Pat, look…" She somehow had to make him see reason. "Shannon was right. Ben's a cop. He may be a dirty one, but he's still a cop, still trained. The first thing he's going to do is check for a wire and a weapon. Then he'll confiscate the weapon, and I'll be left defenseless."

"As much as it pains me to say it—" Jack winced and wilted beneath Pat's stare, then cleared his throat "—she's right, man."

Pat slammed out of the SUV without a word.

Rachel ruffled Shadow's fur and kissed his head. "I'll be back, boy." *God willing.*

"Don't worry, Rachel, we'll find a way to keep an eye on you, and we'll find Jane." Jack reached over to give her hand a reassuring squeeze as she started to slide out of the back seat.

She turned her hand over to grip his. "Thank you."

Pat was staring at her when she closed the door and stood shivering.

She pulled the gun from her pocket and held it out to him. "It's the best way, Pat."

He scowled but took the weapon and the extra ammo she offered. "Try not to let him get too close to you. And stay in the clearing so Jack can keep an eye on you."

"Jack?" Rachel's insides went cold. What had she missed? Wasn't Pat going to have her back? That's what she got for trusting that the two of them would work out a coherent plan while she'd indulged in a few moments of blessed silence.

"Jack's going to follow you in. He'll stay to the woods,

hidden but close, while I take Shadow and search for Jane."

It wasn't a bad plan, actually, but she still would have preferred to have Pat watching over her.

He seemed to understand her hesitance. "It'll be okay, Rachel. I've known Jack most of my life. He's my closest friend, and he'd do anything to protect you."

Rachel only nodded, afraid if she spoke, the tremors in her voice would betray her disappointment.

"Shadow has to work with me. It'll be the safest and fastest way to find Jane and get you out of there." He gripped her upper arms, held her tightly. "But as soon as we ascertain if the girl is in the area and get her to safety, if possible, we're coming back for you. So, whatever conversation you feel the need to have with your cousin, I suggest you do so quickly."

"Thank you, Pat. Not only for trusting me and having my back but for understanding why I have to do this." Rachel laid a hand against his cheek, then stood on her tiptoes and kissed his other cheek. "It'll be okay. I'll be okay."

When she started to pull her hand back, he laid his over hers against his face. "I don't like the idea of you going in unarmed."

"I'm not going in unarmed." She stepped back, lowered their joined hands to rest over his heart and smiled. "I've got my secret weapon right here."

"Rachel."

"What? You said I could trust you, and now I am." She gripped his hand tighter. "But you have to trust me as well. I've got this. I have to talk to him. Just talk.

Who knows? Maybe he'll even do the right thing. Either way, I have to try. If there's any chance to save Jane, maybe even save Ben, I have to take it. I can't spend the rest of my life looking back and feeling like I failed either of them."

"I know you can't." He leaned down, then brushed his lips against her cheek.

She wanted more than anything to lean into the kiss, to say forget it, let's go back to the beach where the sunset had seemed so warm and appealing, spend the evening sitting, talking, getting to know one another. Instead, she turned and walked away before she could change her mind.

Rather than beat herself up over a decision that was already made, she allowed her mind to wander as she walked. She knew Jack would be close, because Pat had said he would be, but she didn't see him, didn't hear him, didn't even sense him. Chills raced through her, though the sweat dripping down her back made her think they probably had nothing to do with the cold.

When she reached the clearing where the abandoned shack stood, she stopped. Everything seemed deserted. Had Ben been there and left already? She pulled her cell phone from her pocket and checked the time. Five minutes short of the hour he'd given her. Five extra minutes she could have spent with Pat.

"I have to admit, I wasn't sure you'd come." Ben stepped from the shadows cast by the pine trees.

"Honestly, I wasn't either," she said.

When he started toward her, she took a step back.

He spread his empty hands wide. "I need you to trust me, Rachel."

"I did once."

He grinned, and for just a moment, she could envision the boy he'd been still had a place inside the man. "I was really hoping you'd back off. But I guess I knew you wouldn't. You always were a tenacious little thing."

"One of us had to be." She hated the bitterness in her own voice, hated the blame she cast upon him for failing Rebecca. And yet, she couldn't help feeling he'd betrayed them both.

He nodded, and the grin disappeared. "I'm sorry about Rebecca. Sorry I couldn't save her or get justice for her. For you."

Rage burned in her gut. "Did you even try?"

He moved closer.

Rachel shook her head and took another step back. She wanted desperately to look around and be sure Jack had her covered, see if Pat had found Jane, but she didn't dare. Instead, she kept her gaze firmly locked on Ben. She had to buy Pat enough time for Shadow to find the girl. She lifted her hands, let them drop. "You know what, Ben, it doesn't even matter anymore."

And it surprised her to realize it didn't. She'd counted on him, depended on him to do as he'd promised and find Rebecca and then her killer, but he'd been nothing more than a child himself. Her own guilt had masked the fact that the task had been too daunting, an unattainable goal. And finally, after all the years she'd suffered, some of the anger dissipated.

Rachel let go of the past and turned her attention to

what did still matter: the girl she might still be able to save. "You said you knew where Jane was, that I'd have time to save her. How?"

He looked around, gestured her closer.

She leaned in.

"I was hoping it wouldn't come to this, Rachel."

"To what?"

"I'm sorry."

Movement from behind her caught her attention, but before she could whirl toward her attacker, pain exploded through her head. Blackness encroached in her peripheral vision as she started to fall. A myriad of voices followed her into oblivion.

Pat followed Shadow deeper into the woods. He'd already crept to the back of the shack where Jane had originally been kept to give Shadow her scent. Ideally, he'd have preferred to go to the vacation cabin where Jane had lain in the bed and have Shadow scent the sheets she'd used, but since that had gone up in flames, it only left the shack where Rachel had found her.

Shadow did have her scent, and Pat would follow through, but he had a strong suspicion from the direction they were headed, Shadow was following the trail she and Rachel had fled down.

Rachel. How could he have let her go meet with Ben alone? What had she been thinking? What had he? Whatever it was, he regretted it as he followed Shadow through the iced-over trail. Even though he hadn't spotted any of Golino's men when he went into the shack, he was still uneasy. A sound caught his attention, and he paused. "Shadow, heel."

In work mode, and used to following commands, Shadow trotted back to him and stood at his side. The big dog, his partner as well as family, looked up at him and waited.

Pat closed his eyes and listened to the quiet. Other than Shadow panting and his own harsh breathing, he heard nothing.

And then it came again, the bird call he recognized from their days playing manhunt in the woods surrounding the old McAvey estate when they were kids—the alert that meant Pat should come to Jack.

Rachel!

He ran toward the sound and gestured for Shadow to follow. When he'd almost reached the shack, he paused, crouched behind a tree and waited.

"Psst." Jack emerged from behind a wide oak, Pat's shotgun at the ready. The instant he was sure it was Pat, he lowered the weapon. "He's got her, Pat."

"Rachel?" There was no time to beat himself up. That would have to wait until later.

Jack nodded. "He hit her over the head, knocked her out. I'd've taken the shot, but his minions swarmed out of the woods like cockroaches and helped him get her onto an ATV. They were moving slowly, so we should be able to track them."

Pat nodded and gestured for Jack to move ahead. He instantly fell back on his training, pushing all emotions to the background. He ignored his thundering heart rate and the churning in his gut, dismissed the feeling he shouldn't have let her go alone, and refused to accept the fact that she could be lost to him. But for that one moment, that exact instant when he realized she was in trouble, his world had fallen apart, and all the reasons he'd told himself he never wanted a relationship ceased to matter.

Jack held out the scarf she'd been wearing. "I grabbed this from the SUV when I realized we'd have to search for her."

Pat ignored the dread in the pit of his stomach as he took it from him, led Shadow to the center of the clearing where Jack indicated she'd been taken and held the scarf out for Shadow to scent. "Shadow, find."

It only took a few seconds for him to catch her scent and start moving along the tracks the ATV had left behind.

Pat hung back with Jack to let Shadow lead. "Did you see Jane?"

"No, I don't think she was ever here," Jack said. "I think it was just a setup to grab Rachel."

And they'd fallen for it. Pat never should have agreed to her plan.

"Hey." Jack laid a hand on his arm. "We had to try, Pat. You know that."

Knowing Jack's words were true didn't make it any easier to accept the situation. "I should have tried to talk her out of it."

"If you thought it was the right thing to do, you would have."

"If I'd realized—" He caught himself in time to stop the words that almost slipped out. If he'd realized how much he'd come to care for her in such a short amount of time, realized he wanted something more with her than just a partnership or even a friendship, he'd have insisted they find a different way. As it was, his own stubbornness had possibly cost him any chance of winning her heart.

"She'll be okay, Pat. It's not easy to keep an unconscious passenger upright on an ATV. They were moving slowly with Rachel slumped in front of Ben and probably not going far, or they'd have used an SUV."

Pat nodded his agreement. "How many men did you see?"

"Six. All armed." Jack held out a hand to stop him. "Pat, if I could have gotten a clear shot, I'd have taken him out."

Pat clapped him on the back. "I know, Jack. It's not your fault."

"Or yours."

They started to move again, their flashlight beams picking their way through the woods on Shadow's heels.

Shadow lifted his tail, sniffed in a small circle.

Pat's flashlight beam fell on a cell phone, and he bent to retrieve it. "Rachel's."

"So much for asking Gabe to track her that way." Jack tucked his own phone back into his pocket. "Not that I can get service out here."

"Why don't you go to the car, see if you can get cell phone service and call Gabe, let him know what happened?" Pat held on to hope that if Ben had planned to kill Rachel, he'd have done so in the clearing. The fact that he hadn't must mean he wanted something from her. What, Pat had no idea, but if it bought him time to find her, he'd be grateful.

"If I leave and you don't get cell service back, no one will be able to find you or Rachel. I'll stick around until we have an idea where they're taking her, then I'll go for help. You do realize Gabe was going to put together a team anyway, right?"

Pat nodded. He'd counted on just that. Even though he was desperate to get help for Rachel and Jane, he had to think clearly. He was a trained rescue worker, and Shadow was a trained tracking dog who could also be used in search and rescue if they had a place last seen. He couldn't let the fact that he was in lo—uh…attracted to Rachel hinder his ability to do his job.

And when this was done, he was going to take a couple of days to visit Uncle Finn in Florida, maybe ask Rachel to accompany him since she'd said she would like to meet him, and then it was time, past time, to go back to work at Seaport Fire and Rescue. Even if the sudden sense of purpose hadn't returned to him, the fact that his friends and fellow firefighters jumped to help, not only him but two strangers as well, would have told him all he needed to know about his path in life. And did that path include Rachel? He didn't know, but he did know he wanted the chance to find out.

Shadow angled toward the beach, moving faster along the sand where the water kept the snow from accumulating.

Pat increased his pace, checked his cell phone for service. Yes! Finally.

"I've got it, Pat." Jack fell back to call in reinforcements.

Shadow pulled ahead, and Pat hurried to catch up, jogging along the shoreline through the wet sand where the bay water lapped against the shore, erasing any sign of the ATV's tracks moments after it passed.

Pat shone the flashlight along the beach, careful not to wade too deeply into the water, but aware the ATV could turn up the beach at any time. When he spotted two sets of tire tracks leaving the water's edge and heading up the beach, he paused, inhaled a deep lungful of frigid air and coughed.

Jack clapped him on the back. "Which way do you want to go?"

"Shadow has a scent and is following. He didn't even hesitate when the tracks veered off."

"Okay then, I'll tell you what: you stick with Shadow, and I'll follow these tracks."

Pat nodded and struggled to catch his breath. Moving so quickly in the cold had not only left him winded but achy too. "Gabe?"

"On his way." With one last slap on the back, Jack took off up the beach, following the tracks into the dunes.

Pat inhaled one last deep breath and set off after Shadow. It didn't take long for the dog to return to him, prancing in circles.

"Show me," Pat said, acknowledging Shadow's report. He followed the big dog along the beach as the shoreline curved sharply inward. As he rounded the point, he stopped short. Enormous boulders stacked high along the beach blocked their forward progress.

No way could anyone have gotten over those rocks on an ATV.

When Shadow nudged his leg, Pat looked down at him. "Which way, boy?"

Shadow turned and started up the beach toward a mansion sitting on a patch of high ground. No light spilled from the dark windows or the outdoor floodlights. But Pat trusted Shadow implicitly, so he followed and found one ATV tucked behind the rocks and a trail of footprints leading over the dunes toward the mansion.

Pat flipped his flashlight off. "Stop."

Shadow followed the command and looked up at Pat, awaiting further instructions.

"Down," Pat whispered as he crouched beside the stairway leading up to the back decking.

Movement among the shadows ahead had him hesitating. With no moonlight and no artificial light, he couldn't tell what was moving. Could it be Jack? Possibly, if the ATV tracks he'd followed had led to the same place, but he couldn't be sure. Gabe? No. Definitely not. He'd have had to be waiting right down the road to have arrived so quickly after Jack's call. So, who then?

Golino's men, most likely. Which meant there was a good chance Jane and Rachel were both being held at the seaside mansion. He had to find a safe place to leave Shadow since he couldn't take him into what could well turn into a gunfight. He tucked the flashlight into his pocket and pulled out Rachel's gun. No way he wanted to shoot anyone, but if there was even the slightest chance Rachel was being held in that building, nothing could keep him out.

TEN

Rachel's eyes fluttered open. The thick boldly colored oriental carpet beneath her cheek momentarily disoriented her. Where was she? Wanting nothing more than to close her eyes again and rid herself of the terrible throbbing throughout her entire head, she fought against the urge. Instinct had her remaining still.

"Wake up." A booted toe nudged her rib.

Giving up the pretense, she rolled onto her back and stared straight up into Ben's angry gaze.

"Get up."

She thought about ignoring him, envisioned standing toe to toe with him and giving him a piece of her mind. She'd wanted so badly to trust him. Despite everything he'd done—every way he'd hurt her, betrayed her—she'd given him a chance, and what had he done? He'd betrayed her. Again.

She'd been right not to trust him. She never should have allowed her resolve to be swayed. And still... A sixteen-year-old girl's life hung in the balance. What was she supposed to do? The argument that she hadn't had a choice didn't hold up for her now, though, not now that she realized how badly she'd wanted to trust Ben, to believe in him.

"I said get up," Ben nudged her again.

She might have done any one of the things she could so clearly imagine if not for the automatic weapon aimed at her chest. So instead of reading him the riot act or slapping him in the face, she rose on shaky legs, straightened and held her hands in the air.

It was then she realized they weren't alone in the room. Carmine Golino lounged behind acres of polished mahogany desk, a cigar clamped between his lips. "Welcome, Ms. Davenport. So nice of you to join us."

She bit back any nasty response when she saw Jane slumped against the wall, eyes closed. Her chest rose and fell in an easy rhythm, and a wave of relief poured through Rachel. The girl was alive, and for now, that's all that mattered. Whatever drug they'd given her to render her unconscious would eventually wear off, and she would heal. At least, she would if Rachel could figure a way out of this mess.

Pat! The name came unbidden along with an image of him standing amid the swirling snow, Shadow at his side. Pat would come for her. Of that she had no doubt. With that absolute certainty came the realization that not everyone couldn't be trusted. Just as her trust in Ben had been misplaced.

Now all she had to do was stall long enough for Pat to find a way to help. And when he did, when they were finally finished with this entire mess—because any other outcome was intolerable—she was going to have a repeat of that kiss on the train. Only this time, it wouldn't be a ruse to distract a gunman. It would be with her whole heart. Because as she stood there trembling in the face of certain death, it was his face that came to her, his arms she wanted to fall into, his help she knew would come. She only prayed it wouldn't be too late.

"Cat got your tongue, dear?" Golino slid his leather chair back from the desk and rose to his full better-than-six-foot height. A bulky man with sagging jowls, a bulbous nose and a designer suit that had probably cost more than she made in an entire month, he pinned her with a cold stare.

She tilted her head, pressed her lips tightly together to keep her teeth from chattering, determined to wait him out. She kept an eye on Ben beside her in her peripheral vision. She'd prefer if he'd move in front of her, didn't like having a threat where she couldn't keep a close watch on him, but at the moment, she perceived Golino as the bigger danger. Even though several weapons lay on his desk, it would only take a second for him to reach them, and even less than that for him to issue the order for Ben to kill her.

Tremors shook her, but still she stood her ground.

"Stubborn little thing, aren't you?" His smile, a wicked baring of teeth, sent a jolt of fear rushing through her. She was in serious trouble. "That's fine, then. But I'm going to need you to answer some questions."

As he rounded the desk, he set his cigar in a glass bowl and picked up one of the automatic weapons from the desk, let it dangle carelessly from his hand as he moved toward her. When he lifted the weapon, instead of aiming at her, he pointed the muzzle toward Jane. "Question one, where's the other girl?"

"I don't know." She cursed her shaky voice.

He sighed, deep and sorrowful. "Wrong answer."

"Wait. Please, I honestly don't know." Her thoughts ricocheted between trying to figure out some kind of escape plan, some way to save Jane and how she could answer his questions without implicating anyone else.

"Okay, I'll give you that one. For now." He took a step closer.

Another few feet, and he'd be within reach. Could she take him? Disarm him? A quick glance told her Ben still had his weapon aimed at her. But would he shoot? Wasn't that the million-dollar question?

"Who's been helping you?" He folded his arms, let the weapon lay across his ample belly. "We already have the fireman."

A vice gripped her chest, squeezed hard.

"At least, we know who he is, and my men will pick him up any moment, probably close by if my intuition is correct, which it usually is."

"Not this time." It was looking less and less likely she'd be able to save herself and Jane, but she would not give up Pat and his friends. If it was the last thing she did, she'd die protecting those who'd risked their own safety to help her. And if the last words she uttered were a lie, hopefully God would understand and forgive her. "He would never have agreed to me meeting with Ben, so I ditched him after Ben called."

Golino pursed his lips, studied her.

She wanted to melt beneath his reptilian gaze. She'd never seen anyone with such empty eyes. This man held not a single ounce of compassion or love. If she ever looked upon pure evil, she had a feeling it would look just like him.

He offered a casual shrug. "No matter, we'll find him either way. But I need to know who else you've told about the girl. It won't do me any good to get rid of you just to have one of your cronies spill the beans, now would it?"

She shook her head in answer, not so much to respond to him as to get a good look at Ben. He held the gun ready, his expression unreadable. She couldn't expect any help from him.

"I didn't tell anyone." She forced herself to stare into his eyes, resisted the urge to shift her gaze.

Golino shifted his weapon, held it leveled at Rachel's chest. "Maybe I underestimated your affection for the girl. I'm going to ask you only once more. Who else knows, and where is the other girl?"

Rachel clenched her teeth together, clamped her lips tight to keep any words trapped inside. Not that she'd ever tell him what he wanted to know, but telling him off would only antagonize him further.

"Very well, then." He lifted the weapon, squeezed the trigger.

Ben hit her from the side even as he stepped in front of her and opened fire.

Rachel staggered and fell to her knees.

Golino's expression finally held some kind of emotion. Shock twisted his features as he went down, hand pressed against the bullet wounds in his chest. The weapon fell from his hand, clattered to the ground.

Ben lay on the carpeted floor a few feet from her. Golino had managed to get off a few shots before he fell, at least two of which hit Ben in the chest.

"Oh, Ben, no." She crawled to him, cradled his head in her lap as her tears flowed freely. "Ben, please, hold on. I'll get help for you."

When she started to lay his head down and stand, he gripped her wrist. "Stay."

She tried to pull away. "I have to call for help."

"I'll do it." Jane wobbled to her feet, staggered toward the desk where Golino's cell phone lay. As she passed Golino, she kicked his weapon farther away from his hand with her foot.

Knowing help would come, Rachel turned her attention to Ben.

"I'm sorry," he wheezed, then dragged in a ragged breath.

"It's okay. Don't worry about it." She sobbed softly. "It doesn't matter now."

Someone pounded on the door.

His hand slid down to hers, gripped it loosely. "I tried, Rachel...tried to find out why he killed her."

"Killed who, Ben?" She scrambled across the floor and grabbed Golino's weapon, then shrugged out of her sweatshirt, applied pressure to the worst of Ben's wounds.

"Rebecca. Tried... I knew he did, but I couldn't prove it. Got close... Needed to know why. Needed proof.

Even thought of just killing him and being done with it, but I couldn't justify it."

Rachel wanted to understand what he was telling her, was torn between listening, administering first aid and keeping an eye on the locked door Golino's men would surely break down any moment. "You shot the men that were after me before you knew it was me they were going to shoot."

"Golino!" The pounding on the door came again, followed by a hard hit.

They didn't have much time before Golino's goons would get in. She applied pressure to Ben's wound with one hand, aimed Golino's weapon at the door with the other.

Jane dropped next to her, took the gun.

Desperately needing to save Ben, Rachel relinquished it without an argument.

"Didn't matter. Didn't want them to kill anyone. When I could stop it, I did." He shuddered with the effort to breathe. "Once I knew it was you, I tried to buy you time to escape without blowing my cover. Worked too hard to let it go. An obsession, I suppose."

"Oh, Ben." She hunched over him, hugging him awkwardly against her as she tried to keep pressure on the wound. "Why didn't you tell me?"

He looked her straight in the eye and grinned. "Like I said, always tenacious. Rebecca had already been robbed of her life. I'd already dedicated mine to trying to find justice for her. I didn't want that for you. Wanted you to find peace."

She rocked back and forth. Pain tore through her, an endless ache that wouldn't be eased.

Silence enveloped them. The pounding on the door had stopped. Would they come at them from another direction?

"Need you...do something," Ben whispered.

She nodded, swiped the tears from her cheeks and gripped his hand. "Okay. I will." It didn't matter what he needed; she'd do it. Anything. She'd been so wrong about him.

He pressed a paper into her hand and whispered. "Go alone."

"Okay, sure, Ben." She glanced at the address jotted on the paper and jammed it into her pocket. She'd deal with it later, but for now, she just needed to get him help. "Did you get the police, Jane?"

"I did, yes. I told them what happened, said we need an ambulance. They're sending help." The whole time she spoke, she held the weapon in a white-knuckled grip and sobbed softly. She kept her wary gaze glued to Golino as if expecting him to jump up and attack.

Rachel squeezed Ben's hand tighter. "Just hold on, Ben. Help's coming."

He looked into her eyes and smiled. "It's okay, Rachel. I might not always have done the right thing, but I did it for the right reason. Love you, kid."

"I love you too, Ben." She rocked him back and forth, begged him to stay with her, to hold on a little longer.

As his eyes fluttered closed, one hard hit had the door flying open, and the world around her erupted into chaos.

Police officers swarmed into the room.

"Help, please," Rachel cried.

And then Pat was there. He crossed the room in a few long strides, fell to his knees on the opposite side of Ben and laid a hand on her shoulder, searched her eyes. "Are you hurt?"

"No, please, Pat."

But Pat had already turned his attention to Ben. He took him gently from Rachel's arms, lay him on the floor, checked his vitals then began CPR.

"Please, Pat." Rachel sobbed, keeping hold of Ben's hand as she scooted out of the way. "You have to save him. He saved my life."

Jack knelt beside her. "I'm here, Pat."

Together, the two worked frantically to save Ben until the paramedics arrived to take over.

When she was forced out of the way, Rachel scrambled back against the wall, her head pounding, a dull ache practically consuming her.

Jane stood wrapped in a blanket with a police officer's arm draped protectively over her shoulders. She looked over at Rachel and mouthed, "Thank you."

Rachel only nodded, relieved the young girl was finally safe.

As the paramedics wheeled Ben out on a gurney, Pat knelt facing her. "Are you okay?"

Tears tracked freely down her cheeks. She sniffed. "I am. Yes."

He gripped both of her hands, pressed his forehead against hers. "When I heard the gunfire in here and couldn't get to you, my heart stopped."

A soft sob escaped. "I'm just glad you're here now."

"I would have come in sooner, but Golino had men outside that had to be dealt with. And there were other women being held here as well."

She nodded, not caring about the specifics, just happy he was with her now. "I was wrong not to trust Ben. He saved my life."

Pat cradled her face between his hands. "Then I owe him a great debt."

"I'm sorry I didn't completely trust you, too. But I want you to know that in the end, I did. I knew you'd come."

"I'm glad." He brushed his lips gently against her forehead. "Now, why don't we get out of here? Jack's been holding the police officers off so I could have a moment with you, but you're going to have to answer their questions, and then what do you say we find somewhere nice and quiet to relax and have dinner? I'm starved."

She laughed as she nodded. "I'd like that."

"And after that, what do you say to a few days in Florida? I'd really like for you to meet Uncle Finn."

Warmth, sunshine and Pat. Sounded like the perfect combination to help her begin to heal. "Sounds like a plan, but not until I know if Ben is going to be okay. Oh, and speaking of Ben, there's something I have to do first. I'd like you to come with me."

With Ben on the mend and Golino's men rounded up and under arrest, Rachel was finally ready to deal with whatever task her cousin needed her help with a few days later. First, though, they had to drop Jane and Shannon off at the airport.

Pat hugged Jane tight, then set her back and kissed her forehead. "You stay safe now. And don't forget you and Shannon are coming to spend a week with us this summer."

She smiled, the first time Pat had ever seen her do so. "How could I forget? You promised to teach me how to sail."

He ruffled her hair, then turned to Shannon and hugged her as well. "You two take care of each other."

She nodded and wiped the tears shimmering in her eyes.

"Hey." He lifted her chin to force her gaze to meet his. "It's going to be fine. Jane's parents were beyond thrilled to have found her."

"And they thanked me about a hundred times on the phone for looking out for her, but…" She sucked in a shaky breath. "Well, it's been a long time since I've been part of a family. I don't know if I remember how."

He wrapped his arm around her shoulders and squeezed, and his gaze landed on Rachel hugging Jane, the two crying openly. "Trust me, it will come naturally. And if you have any problems, you know you can always call me or Rachel. No more running off."

"I will, I promise." She stood on tiptoe and kissed his cheek. "Thank you."

"Anytime, kiddo."

Since they weren't allowed through the gate, Pat and Rachel stood arm in arm and waved goodbye to the two girls from the sidewalk.

They waved back, then held hands as they entered the airport, both nervous about greeting Jane's parents.

Pat glanced at Rachel. "You talked to her parents, right?"

"I did, yes." Rachel still looked after them, even though they'd disappeared inside, where Jane's parents had flown in to take them home to Indiana.

"And they seemed okay with taking Shannon too?" If Pat were honest, he had to admit to a certain amount of nerves too. He wanted the best for both Shannon and Jane, and when Jane's parents had offered to let Shannon come live with them, he'd been thrilled. Especially since she had no family of her own. With Golino gone, he hoped they could move past what had happened and make new, happy lives for themselves.

"Seriously okay. Her parents were so ecstatic when I contacted them, told them I'd found her." She lowered her gaze, but not before he saw the pain etched in her expression. "She'd taken off after having a horrible argument with them, and they never gave up hope of finding her. Kids don't realize most things can be fixed if you just talk them out. Running away is never the answer."

His heart ached for Rachel and the guilt she carried. Maybe it was not only time for Jane and Shannon to move on and heal but Rachel as well. He opened his arms and was thrilled when she slid into them, leaned her head against his chest as if she were made to fit in just that spot. "Hon, you may not have been able to bring Rebecca home, but at least you reunited Jane with her parents and found a home for Shannon. I'd say that's not bad for a few days' work."

"I know." She looked up at him, and his heart melted. "Now, come on. We have one more stop to make before we catch our own flight to Florida to visit Uncle Finn."

Pat followed the GPS toward the address on the paper Ben had given Rachel. Though he'd already asked her about a hundred times, he figured it couldn't hurt to try once more. "Are you sure you don't want to talk to the police first?"

Rachel turned to him from the passenger seat, where she'd been quietly gazing out the window. "I'm sure. Ben said go alone, and I trust him."

"But you're bringing me."

"Because I trust you too. More than anyone."

His heart filled with something he suspected might be love. He wove his fingers between hers in what had become a comfortable gesture over the past few days and lifted her hand to kiss her knuckles. "Did you speak to the doctor today?"

"Hmm?" She seemed distracted, lost in her own thoughts as she watched the miles pass out the window. Not that he blamed her after what she'd been through. "Oh, right, yes. Ben's still in the coma, but he's doing as well as can be expected. Better than, really."

He squeezed her hand in reassurance. "He's a strong man, Rachel. He'll pull through."

"I hope so." She shot him a grin that went straight to his heart. "He has a lot of explaining to do."

Pat laughed. Poor guy better enjoy his rest, because he didn't have a clue what he was in for when he woke up.

He pulled up in front of an in-line ranch on a narrow, wooded lot and parked, then scanned the quiet neighborhood before getting out of the car and walking around to open Rachel's door. He had no clue what to expect, didn't know why Ben would send Rachel to the small house on the quiet dead-end street. Keeping his arm around her, he guided her up the brick walkway and two steps to the front porch.

She looked at him, lower lip caught between her teeth in a nervous gesture he'd come to love, then turned and rang the doorbell.

A muffled voice answered through the closed door. "Who is it?"

"My name is Rachel Davenport, and my cousin Ben Harrison sent me."

The door whipped open, and a petite woman in jeans and a sweater, her blue eyes puffy and red-rimmed from crying grabbed Rachel's arm. "Is he okay? Ben? Please, say it fast."

Rachel took her hand. "He's hurt. He's in a coma, but the doctors say he's going to be okay."

She sobbed. "Oh, thank God. When he didn't come home, I wasn't too worried, because, well, sometimes he can't. But when he didn't text me the code so I'd know he had to stay out, I was so scared. Oh my, what am I thinking? I know better than to stand in the open doorway. Would you come in for a moment while I get my stuff together, tell me what happened to him?" She looked up and down the street before stepping aside for them to enter the small but cheerful living room, then closed the door behind them. "I have to get to the hospital. I don't care if it's safe or not, I have to go to Ben. You can sit if you want."

"That's okay, thank you, but we actually have a flight to catch." Rachel studied the woman. "But I was with Ben when he was hurt. He saved my life. And he gave me this piece of paper and told me to come alone." She handed the woman the paper with her address on it. "I'm sorry, but Ben didn't tell me who you are, and I can't help but feel I should recognize you."

She paled instantly. She clutched the scrap of paper against her chest. "I...uh..."

Pat saw the recognition dawn in Rachel's eyes. "I do know you. You're Gemma Bertolino."

The name rang a bell for Pat, but he couldn't place her.

"Please." Sheer terror vibrated from the woman as she started to back away. "I'm sorry, I—"

"Hey, no." Rachel gripped the woman's hands tighter. "It's okay. Carmine Golino is dead. He can't hurt you now."

"It's over?" Gemma sobbed and fell into Rachel's arms. "It's really over?"

"It's okay. A number of the women Golino abducted were found at the mansion and made statements to the police already, and several of his thugs are scrambling to rat out everyone they can in hopes of reducing their own sentences."

Between that and the statements Shannon and Jane had made, and what Ben would surely say when he woke up, Golino's human trafficking ring had been blown wide open. And internal affairs had already opened an investigation to clean house.

Rachel rubbed soothing circles on her back, trying to calm her. "It is. It's over."

Pat went to the kitchen and filled a glass with water.

By the time he returned, she seemed to have gained control of her emotions. Her hand barely shook as she took the glass from him and thanked him.

He stepped back. "You're the witness who disappeared during Golino's trial?"

"I am, yes. When Golino ordered the hit on me, Ben hid me here. He came to check on me, brought me groceries and whatever else I needed. Sometimes he just came and sat with me, kept me company since even though I was alive, I was basically a prisoner in his home. And somehow, over the past three years, we fell in love. He moved in about a year ago, promised we'd get married if we could ever find a safe way to do so."

"Then I hope we'll be invited to the wedding. I'd love to spend some time getting to know you and reconnecting with Ben." Rachel hugged her, then stepped back. "Do you have a way to the hospital?"

"I do, yes, thank you. Ben left a car in the garage for me in case I ever had to run." She laughed and shook her head. "We had a code for that too."

After a little convincing, Gemma agreed to a police escort to the hospital. Gabe arrived shortly after, though likely not soon enough for Gemma, who was anxious to see Ben. Still, they couldn't be too careful when it came to Gemma's safety. With a final farewell and a promise to keep in touch, Pat and Rachel left.

Rachel looked over her shoulder as they walked to the car. "He kept her safe for three years."

Pat slung an arm around her shoulder. "He's a good man, Rachel. He's going to be okay. They're going to be okay."

"I'm glad."

"Me too." They strolled slowly back to the car, in no hurry since they still had some time before their flight. "You know, I was thinking…"

"Uh-oh."

"Ha ha." He bumped her with a hip.

"Okay, tell me." She leaned her head against his shoulder. "What were you thinking?"

"I was thinking an IT tech, like a journalist, can pretty much work from anywhere."

She looked up at him and lifted a brow. "Oh, you were, were you?"

"Uh-huh. And I'd consider leaving if it's what you want, but I'd really like to stay in Seaport." He didn't want to push her too fast, wanted to let their relationship evolve slowly over time, but he had every intention of marrying this incredible woman, of spending the rest of his life with her. "And since Shadow took to you so well, I feel like he'd miss you if we were apart."

At the mention of his name, Shadow barked from the back seat. When Pat opened the door and let him out, he ran straight to Rachel, nuzzled his head against her hip.

"Hey, no fair." She petted Shadow, and her laughter warmed Pat's heart. "The two of you are teaming up now, conspiring to convince me to…what?"

"Marry me." The words slipped out before he could think to stop them. "Not now… I mean…uh, not yet.

But one of these days. Maybe. I'd like to, you know, eventually—"

"It's okay, Pat." Laughing, she kissed him gently. "For now, why don't we head down to Florida to meet Uncle Finn? And I seem to remember a promise to sit on the beach together—you, me and Shadow—to watch the sun set over the ocean."

He pulled her close, laid a hand on Shadow's head, and everything in his world was suddenly right. "Sounds like the perfect way to spend an evening."

* * * * *

Dear Reader,

Thank you so much for sharing Pat and Rachel's story! I love flawed characters whose internal conflicts are as unique and challenging as the danger they find themselves in.

One of the things both Pat and Rachel struggle with is the ability to trust. They've both been hurt in the past and are having a difficult time learning to trust again. I think all of us go through trials in our lives that make it difficult to open up and trust one another, but as long as we continue to trust in God, I believe we can learn to trust others again.

I hope you've enjoyed sharing Pat and Rachel's journey as much as I enjoyed creating it. If you'd like to keep up with my new stories, you can find me on Facebook (deenaalexanderauthor) and Twitter (@deenaalexander). Or sign up for my newsletter: https://bit.ly/3O7fIHk.

Deena Alexander

HARLEQUIN
PLUS

Try the best multimedia subscription service for romance readers like you!

Read, Watch and Play.

Experience the easiest way to get the romance content you crave.

Start your **FREE TRIAL** at
<u>www.harlequinplus.com/freetrial</u>.